Sh[e] To Find.

Diana's daughter. Destiny's daughter. Suddenly he was thankful that he had allowed his curiosity to lead him to this woman.

She stood on the porch and leaned one shoulder against a post. She was radiant, ethereal, like a daydream. Black, glossy hair fell past her shoulders and framed an oval face. Her eyes were pastel blue, wide, and tilting up at the corners. Her mouth was small, pouty and shapely. A tiny beauty mark rode on her left cheekbone. Just like her mother, he thought.

Her mother. And his father. If she found out who he was, she would ask him to leave, and for that reason he couldn't let her know.

Dear Reader,

Welcome to Silhouette! Our goal is to give you hours of unbeatable reading pleasure, and we hope you'll enjoy each month's six new Silhouette Desires. These sensual, provocative love stories are both believable and compelling—sometimes they're poignant, sometimes humorous, but always enjoyable.

Indulge yourself. Experience all the passion and excitement of falling in love along with our heroine as she meets the irresistible man of her dreams and together they overcome all obstacles in the path to a happy ending.

If this is your first Desire, I hope it'll be the first of many. If you're already a Silhouette Desire reader, thanks for your support! Look for some of your favorite authors in the coming months: Stephanie James, Diana Palmer, Dixie Browning, Ann Major and Doreen Owens Malek, to name just a few.

Happy reading!

Isabel Swift
Senior Editor

ELAINE CAMP
Destiny's Daughter

Silhouette Desire
Published by Silhouette Books New York
America's Publisher of Contemporary Romance

SILHOUETTE BOOKS
300 East 42nd St., New York, N.Y. 10017

Copyright © 1986 by Deborah Camp

All rights reserved, including the right to reproduce
this book or portions thereof in any form whatsoever.
For information address Silhouette Books,
300 East 42nd St., New York, N.Y. 10017

ISBN: 0-373-05298-7

First Silhouette Books printing August 1986

All the characters in this book are fictitious. Any
resemblance to actual persons, living or dead, is
purely coincidental.

SILHOUETTE, SILHOUETTE DESIRE and colophon
are registered trademarks of the publisher.

America's Publisher of Contemporary Romance

Printed in the U.S.A.

Books by Elaine Camp

Silhouette Romance

To Have, To Hold #99
Devil's Bargain #173
This Tender Truce #270

Silhouette Desire

Love Letters #207
Hook, Line And Sinker #251
Destiny's Daughter #298

Silhouette Special Edition

For Love Or Money #113
In A Pirate's Arms #159
Just Another Pretty Face #263
Vein Of Gold #285
Right Behind the Rain #301
After Dark #316

ELAINE CAMP

dreamed of becoming a writer for many years. Once she tried it she quickly became successful, perhaps due to her reporter's eye, which gives her a special advantage in observing human relationships.

One

"I hope they give me Clover again. He's my favorite horse!"

The excited voice of the child piped above the other voices on the minibus, and Yuri Zaarbo winced and stared stoically out the grimy window at the distant green hills. He wished he were back in Houston, back at NASA, back where he belonged. Idle pleasure, vacations, playing cowboys and Indians...well, they weren't his style. So what was he doing on a bus headed for Rocking Horse Dude Ranch in the heart of Oklahoma?

He caught his reflection in the glass and erased the disgruntled scowl from his face. Make the best of it, he told the dark-haired, dark-eyed man. Only in America would employers force their employees to take vacations.

"Yuri, your work will still be here when you get back," the head of his project had told him. "You need a vacation. All work and no play makes Jack a dull boy."

Jack a dull boy? Yuri frowned again, thinking that some of the American sayings—especially in Texas—were very odd. Very odd, indeed. Who was this Jack, anyway?

"Is this your first visit to Rocking Horse?" the man seated beside him asked, drawing Yuri's attention from his reflection in the window.

"Yes," he answered, glancing at the passenger who had introduced himself earlier as Frank Ferguson. He was married to the woman across the aisle and his daughter was the one with the banshee voice.

"This is our fifth year in a row," Frank said with a boastful grin. "You'll love it. It's like being in the middle of a John Wayne movie."

Yuri managed a tight smile.

"Do you like to ride?" Frank asked, intent on drawing Yuri into a conversation.

"Not really." Yuri shrugged at Frank's surprised look. "I decided to come here for... for other reasons."

"The clear air, right? I hear that Houston has a smog problem."

"Yes, like many American cities." Scenes of Moscow flitted through his mind, and he looked at the window again to examine the melancholy in his dark eyes. "But Houston has other things to offer besides pollution," he added, defending his new home and his decision to defect to America. "It's a friendly place, an exciting place."

"Oh, sure," Frank agreed. "What sort of work do you do?"

"I work for NASA."

"That right?" Frank glanced over at his wife. "Honey, our Russian friend here works for the space program!"

"How exciting! Are you an astronaut?"

Yuri smiled, wishing he had a dollar for every time he'd been asked that recently. "No, an aerodynamics engineer."

"How long have you been in America?" Flo Ferguson asked, leaning forward to look past her husband at Yuri.

"Almost two years."

"You speak English so well," Frank observed.

"I was fluent in it before I arrived here." Yuri breathed a sigh of relief when the minibus rolled under a sign that proclaimed that they had entered the Rocking Horse compound. The attention immediately switched from Yuri to the rustic house in the distance.

"There it is!" Fawn Ferguson shrieked, pointing a chubby finger toward the house. "Wocking Horse Wanch!"

Yuri hid his smile behind his hand. Frank, Flo and Fawn Ferguson. How excruciatingly cute.

The minibus came to a stop in front of the log and mortar house and deposited its passengers. Yuri claimed his two pieces of luggage, then examined the woman who greeted them. She was a disappointment. He'd expected to see a family resemblance, but she looked nothing like the pictures he'd seen of her mother. This woman had red curly hair and green eyes instead of the dark hair and blue eyes he'd imagined for her. She must favor her father's side of the family.

"Welcome to Rocking Horse," the woman said with a cheery smile. "Let me call roll and then we'll get you settled in." She ticked off the names, then paused to concentrate on the paper in her hands.

Yuri smiled, realizing that it was his name that baffled her. He reminded himself that he'd registered under his mother's maiden name, then wondered if he were courting disaster by not revealing his true identity.

"Your-ee My-TOE-vah," he said, pronouncing it slowly for her.

She smiled her thanks. "Yuri Mytova," she repeated. "That's a mouthful. By the way, for those of you who haven't met me before, I'm DiDi Adams."

DiDi Adams? Yuri's brows shot up and a smile tipped up one corner of his mouth. She wasn't Diana's daughter! Sweet relief flowed through him, but it was fleeting. Where was she then? Had she sold the ranch to someone else? He stared at the tips of his leather loafers, thinking that he might have come here for nothing. Two weeks! He'd have to stay here two weeks and she wasn't even here any—

"Hello, everyone."

The melodic voice arrested him. His heart sputtered, his pulse rate accelerated and his gaze moved slowly, hopefully, to the woman who had spoken. The sight of her made his breath catch in his throat.

Ah, yes. She was what he'd expected to find. Diana's daughter. Suddenly, he was glad to be on vacation and thankful that he had allowed his curiosity to lead him to this woman.

She stood on the porch and leaned one shoulder against a support. She was radiant, ethereal, like a daydream. Black, glossy hair fell past her shoulders and framed an oval face. Her eyes were pastel blue, wide and tilting up at the corners. Her mouth was small, pouty and shapely. A tiny beauty mark rode on her left cheekbone. Just like her mother, he thought.

She moved down the steps, slim and lissome in jeans and a voluminous white shirt that was tucked into a narrow waistband. Her smile was friendly if slightly aloof. There was something regal about the way she moved, the way her gaze swept over the faces of her guests. She was a queen addressing her court.

"I'm Banner O'Bryan," she said, confirming what Yuri already knew. "I'm the owner of Rocking Horse Dude Ranch and I hope you enjoy your time with us."

"Can I have Clover as my horse?" Fawn Ferguson asked, moving to Banner and tugging her sleeve.

"Yes, you may," Banner said, her smile warming and growing more sincere as she ran a slender hand over the girl's head. "It's nice to see you again, Fawn." She looked up from the child's adoring smile and addressed the others again. "First things first. If you'll all come inside, DiDi will assign cabins and tell you about our itinerary." She stepped back, one arm arcing in a sweeping gesture toward the main house. The new arrivals obeyed like loyal subjects.

Yuri started past her, then stopped, unwilling to play by her rules of conduct. "Excuse me, Miss O'Bryan, but I was—"

"Banner," she interrupted. "We're on a first-name basis here."

"Banner," he said, wondering how she'd come by that name. Did it have some significance? "I'm Yuri Mytova." He shook hands with her, noticing the tense set of her lips when the origin of his name registered in her mind.

"Yuri," she said. "That's Russian, or maybe Polish?"

"Russian. I'm a naturalized American citizen."

She pulled her hand from his as if his touch made her uneasy. She folded her arms at her waist and waited for him to continue.

"I was wondering if you take part in the activities here," Yuri said, intrigued by her wary reaction to him. Did she hold a grudge? Did she harbor a prejudice against anything or anyone Russian?

"Yes, I'm into everything around here." Her eyes narrowed slightly. "Why do you ask?"

He shrugged off her question and started up the steps to the porch. "I was wondering if you were a figurehead or a real..." He paused at the top step and glanced over his shoulder at her. His pitchy gaze swept from her head to her feet. "Cowgirl," he finished with a smirk.

"Cowgirl?" Banner repeated, unsure as to whether she should be insulted or amused. She didn't like the way he was looking at her, sizing her up with those dark eyes of his. It made her nervous, so she laughed softly and looked down at her cabin list. "Just think of me as your hostess."

"Do you aim to please?"

She angled a glance at him, wondering what kind of game he was playing. Lowering the clipboard, she turned to face him fully. "Our aim is to make your vacation memorable."

"It already is," he said, then strode into the house.

Banner shook her head, perplexed by him. Russians! she thought, smiling to herself. Did all Russian men think they were irresistible? She found his name on her list. Yuri Mytova. He was an attractive man, she allowed, but he wasn't irresistible. Not to her, anyway. She wouldn't have any trouble resisting his dark, shining eyes and come-hither smile.

She walked over to the corral and rested one arm on the top railing. Forcing thoughts of the Russian from her mind, she watched the horses in the corral kick up their heels and nip playfully at each other, almost as if they were putting on a show for her.

Show-offs, she thought, then sighed when she realized that she was thinking of that Russian again. He was a show-off. She could tell that just by the way he walked; he was arrogant and self-assured. Had Vladimir been like that? she wondered, then brought herself up short. Comparisons were not only unfair but a form of self-torture, and she'd tortured herself enough over Vladimir and Diana. Just because a Russian had been responsible for the breakup of her parents' marriage didn't give her the right to blame the entire Soviet Union!

Banner turned around to face the house and, as if on cue, Yuri Mytova pushed open the screen door and stepped onto the porch. Banner tensed as his gaze locked with hers, but she remained perfectly still, refusing to be intimidated by him. A ray of sunlight fell upon his face and she could see his lazy smile of appraisal. He lifted one hand in a brief salute before leaving the sheltering porch and striding in the direction of the guest cabins. Banner released her breath in a long sigh as she observed his fluid walk, his arms swinging slightly at his sides, his shoulders swaying with a hint of male bravado, his carriage straight and proud.

She whipped her gaze in the opposite direction and found herself staring at her foreman.

"Pete!" She placed a hand to her heart. "You scared me."

"Sorry." Pete stuffed his fingers in the back pockets of his jeans. He looked past her and smiled. "It's good to be back at work again, isn't it? I'm sure looking forward to the trail ride tomorrow, aren't you?"

"I think I'll make myself scarce," Banner said, glancing in the direction the Russian had taken.

"What?" Pete dipped his head to see her expression. "Why? What's wrong?"

"Oh, nothing." She kicked at a tuft of spring grass. She didn't want to reveal to Pete her loathing for dark Russians. He wouldn't understand, and it was none of his business. It was personal. "Guess I'm just getting lazy. I might let you handle the trail rides by yourself."

"Banner O'Bryan," Pete chided her, "what's gotten into you? Are you sick or something? You've always loved the trail rides."

"I know, I know." She pushed herself from the fence. "Don't pay any mind to me. I'm just in a lousy mood."

"Hey, did you hear about that Russian fella?"

Banner whirled back to Pete. "What about him?"

"He works for NASA in Houston." Pete grinned, looking boyish and much younger than his thirty-four years. "Wonder if he's been on the moon?"

She'd like to send him to the moon, Banner thought, smiling at the notion.

"You sure you're feeling all right?"

"I'm fine." She looked toward the house. "I've got a case of spring fever, that's all."

"Well, you've had it all winter," Pete observed dryly. "You're usually excited to see the first guests arrive, but this season is different. Are you getting itchy feet?"

"No, of course not. Itchy feet for what? This is my home, Pete. Why would I want to leave it?"

"Wouldn't blame you if you wanted to venture out in the world. Now that Luke's gone there's nothing holding you here."

"Nothing but my livelihood," she noted. She looked around distractedly, uneasy with the conversation because it was hitting too close to home. She had been restless lately. There was a yearning in her, a yearning that wouldn't go away. "Now that the season has started I'll get back into the swing of things," she said, more for herself than for Pete.

"I could run the place if you wanted to get away for a while," Pete offered, giving her a shy glance. "I mean, I wouldn't mind a bit."

"Are you trying to get rid of me, Pete Parker?"

"No!" He smiled and chucked her playfully under the chin. "All I'm saying is that nobody would blame you if you had a yen to see other places."

"This place has always been enough for me," she said, lifting her chin with stubborn determination. "It always will be."

Pete nodded, but his eyes reflected concern. "Okay, hon. Are you serious about not going on the trail rides?"

"I don't know." She shrugged, wishing she could be decisive and not so wishy-washy. "I'll let you know."

Yuri stood back from the cabin for a few minutes, taking in its rustic facade before he went inside to examine the homespun decor.

"Early American," he said, crossing the oval rug to the bedroom area where he deposited his luggage. A patchwork quilt was draped across the four-poster bed and a vase of wildflowers adorned the bedside table.

He stood by the window while he examined the map DiDi had given him.

Rocking Horse resort was larger than he'd imagined it would be. There were ten cabins and a circle of buildings for the guests' use; there was a dry-goods store, a leather-goods store, a restaurant and a place called Shortbranch Saloon and Dance Hall. These buildings were referred to as "the town." The map also pointed out fishing holes, stables and corrals. Bridle trails meandered all over the property, each given a colorful Western name: Horseshoe, Maverick, Lasso and Branding Iron Trails.

"How quaint," Yuri said with a grimace. "Makes me want to hop on my faithful steed and ride the range."

It was stupid to come here, he scolded himself. He had no interest in cowboys and Western villages. Bridle trails, indeed! If he never rode a horse again, it would be too soon. He was crazy to come here.

A self-derisive grin overtook him, and he turned from the window to open the smaller of his two suitcases. Tucked among his shirts was a book—his father's diary. He stroked the red leather cover, remembering his father's descriptions of Diana Dufrayne O'Bryan. Opening it, he removed a dog-eared photo and examined Diana's face. His thumb moved across the beauty mark on Diana's cheekbone. Like mother, like daughter.

Banner's reaction to his being Russian interested him. She must hold a ton of resentment within her, he mused. She must be as bitter as he had been before he'd read the diary and had grown to understand the reasons behind his father's defection and his relationship with Diana.

Yuri sat on the bed and flipped through the volume, recalling how surprised he'd been to learn that his father had kept a personal diary. It wasn't until Yuri had arrived in America that he'd been told that his father had been dead two years. Two years, and none of the family had been notified.

A friend of his father's had given him a few of Vladimir Zaarbo's personal items; a gold watch, Vlad's conducting baton and this diary. The contents of the diary had astonished Yuri. Such passion, such poetic verve! The words flowed and tore at the heart with the depth of their feeling and their understanding of the things Yuri had gone through while he'd lived in Russia. The parallels between himself and his father staggered him, leaving no doubt that Vladimir and Yuri had been cut from the same cloth.

He was his father's son, but was Banner her mother's daughter? Did she possess Diana's fiery spirit and passionate nature?

Ah yes, he thought. That's why he'd chosen this place for his vacation, to find the answer to that question. In a way, he'd fallen in love with Diana through his father's diary, and he couldn't help but wonder if Diana's daughter might be the woman of his dreams.

He fell back on the bed, letting the diary slip from his fingers. First, he'd have to get past Banner's frosty coating of prejudice, he decided. If the fire was there it lay behind the iciness of her smile.

Restlessness stirred within him, making him wish for his work again. Work was good for the soul, but this silly mission of his wasn't. Why should he care about Banner O'Bryan? Granted, she was a beautiful woman, but America was full of them.

He gave a resigned sigh. He was here, he told himself, so he should make the best of it. Sleep edged into his mind as he closed his eyes and wondered where Banner O'Bryan rested her head when the moon was high.

"Got a minute?" DiDi asked as she stepped into Banner's office.

"Sure. What's up?" Banner closed the ledger and leaned back in the chair that had been her father's.

"The funniest thing," DiDi said, giggling as she dropped into one of the chairs in front of the desk. "That Russian guy... Yuri?"

"Yes, what about him?"

"He called the switchboard right before dinner and asked for room service!" DiDi placed a hand against her stomach as her giggles grew into peals of laughter. "Room service! Isn't that a hoot?"

"Where does he think he is?" Banner asked. "The Waldorf?"

"I don't know, but he was surprised when I said we didn't have room service. I explained that dinner was at seven in the dining room. He asked if a drink couldn't be sent to his room, and I told him that we didn't do that kind of thing here. If he wanted a drink he could go over to the Shortbranch." DiDi shrugged helplessly. "I think he was miffed. He hung up without so much as a 'thank you kindly.'"

"Hmmm." Banner tapped the eraser end of the pencil against her nose in contemplation. "I suspected that he didn't belong in a place like this. Wonder why he decided to vacation here."

"I don't know, but he's barking up the wrong tree."

The phone buzzed at Banner's elbow and she reached out to answer it. "Banner O'Bryan, may I help you?"

"Yes, this is Yuri."

Banner felt her eyes widen and she placed one hand over the mouthpiece. "It's him," she whispered to DiDi, then removed her hand. "Yes, Yuri. What can I do for you?"

"Could I drop by in a few minutes and talk with you?"

Banner winked at DiDi. "Sure. Is there a problem?"

"I'll be there in ten minutes."

"Well!" Banner stared at the receiver for a moment before she placed it in its cradle. "He just hung up!"

"He does that," DiDi said with a frown. "Rude, huh?"

"Very rude." Banner cleared off the top of her desk, wanting to present a neat and orderly presence for Yuri Mytova. "There's something about that man that's infuriating."

"Yes, and that's too bad." DiDi stood up and moved toward the door. "I always thought Russians were romantic, sentimental, passionate!"

"Whatever gave you that idea?" Banner asked, throwing DiDi a baffled look.

"I've seen movies about them. Remember *Dr. Zhivago*?"

"That's fiction, not fact," Banner pointed out. "Besides, an Egyptian played the part of Dr. Zhivago in the movie. Maybe Egyptians are romantic, sentimental and passionate, but I've always thought that Russians were sneaky, cold and immoral."

DiDi turned slowly to face her. "You're thinking about that Russian and your mother, aren't you?"

"No!" Banner realized that she was standing, having shot up from the chair as if she'd received an electrical shock. She stared at DiDi—DiDi, who had been her best friend for six years but had never let on that she knew about Diana and Vladimir. "Who told you about them?"

"Lucas," DiDi said, leaning back against the door with an outward calm. "He never made any bones about it. He said your mother left him and took up with a Russian composer."

"Dad told you that?" Banner shook her head, unable to believe that her father would talk about it with DiDi and skirt the subject with his own daughter. "I find that hard to believe, DiDi. Dad rarely spoke about Diana to me."

"Maybe that's because you didn't want to hear what he had to say about your mother and her Russian defector."

The need to protect herself grew strong within Banner, but her curiosity won out. "What did he tell you?"

"That he didn't blame Diana for leaving," DiDi said nonchalantly.

"That's not true!" Banner's hands balled into fists at her sides. "Of course he blamed her! She left him. He loved her desperately and she left him!"

DiDi shrugged again. "It happens. All marriages aren't made in heaven, hon. I mean, it's not like she left Luke for another man. Lucas said that they separated, she went to New York, the divorce was finalized and then she met Vladimir Zaarbo."

"That was her story, but I don't believe it. She'd made several trips to New York before she told my father she was leaving for good. I think she met that...that...Zaarbo *before* she decided to leave her husband and child."

"Maybe that's what you want to believe. Maybe you want to blame someone so you've decided to make your mother a vamp. Luke said that he didn't have any hard feelings for Diana. He said she did what she had to do."

"That's a lie!"

DiDi's green eyes narrowed. "You calling me a liar, Banner?"

"No." Banner took a deep breath, warning herself not to wound her friend. "I'm just saying that you misunderstood. When my mother left Dad, he was devastated. Dad was a good, gentle man and Diana left him for an egotistical, self-centered foreigner."

"Russian, you mean," DiDi said with an understanding smile. "Banner, they're not all bad guys. Personally, I think that Yuri is a nice enough fella. He could improve on his manners, but—"

A knock sounded on the other side of the door and DiDi jumped forward in alarm. Smiling at herself, she turned back to Banner with a question in her eyes.

"Yes, let him in," Banner said, then reached out and squeezed DiDi's hand. "I'm sorry. When I talk about this I get all worked up. Forgive me?"

"Don't worry about it," DiDi reassured her. "No offense was taken."

DiDi opened the door to Yuri, then eased past him and closed the door behind her.

Yuri glanced over his shoulder, then back to Banner. "I'm interrupting?"

"No, it's nothing." She motioned toward one of the chairs. "Have a seat," she said lightly, then went back to the chair behind the desk. "DiDi told me that you seemed confused about our operation here."

"Confused?" He paused, then shook his head. "No." He sat down, crossed one leg over the other and removed a pack of cigarettes from his shirt pocket. "Disappointed?" His gaze met hers briefly over the flame of his lighter. "Yes."

Banner glared at his impassive, handsome face and wanted to apply the back of her hand to it. "If you're disappointed then it might be because you expected something other than what we offer. This is a dude ranch, not a luxury resort."

He glanced around the small office as smoke curled above his head. "Do you live here?"

Banner released a weary sigh. "Yes, but what does that have to do with—"

"You have living quarters back there?" he interrupted, pointing his cigarette at the door behind her.

"Yes. Yuri, would you like me to refund your deposit? I'd be happy to do that for you. There are other resorts in this area, and I'm sure you can find accommodations at one of them."

"Are you dismissing me, Banner?" A wicked grin tipped up one side of his mouth. "Am I too much trouble for you? Too much to handle, so to speak?" He leaned forward, offering her a cigarette from his pack. "Would you care for one?"

"I don't like cigarettes," Banner said, her voice frosty as she touched the Thank You For Not Smoking sign on the corner of her desk. "As you can see."

He dipped his head in acknowledgement. "I'm sorry. I didn't notice that or I wouldn't have lit up." He rose to his feet, went behind her to the window, opened it and flicked the cigarette into the night. "I forgot that I'm way out west and people here prefer to chew tobacco instead of smoking it."

Banner bit her lower lip, cautioning herself not to be drawn into a duel with him. "I don't like tobacco in any form."

"I have a sign on my desk at work that says Thank You For Not Breathing While I Smoke." He chuckled, but she didn't.

"Smoking can kill you," she said, staring straight ahead and wishing he'd stop standing behind her.

"So can horses."

Banner counted to ten before she said, "Do you want a refund or not?"

"No, thank you." He moved around the desk and sat down again. "How long have you owned this place?"

"It's been in my family for three generations," she said with pronounced indulgence. "We haven't had any casualties among our guests. Our horses are gentle."

"Has it always been a . . . a dude ranch?"

"No, my father started the dude ranch sixteen years ago. Before that it was a working ranch. A cattle ranch. If you want the history of the place we have a brochure in the lobby that—"

"Why aren't you going on the trail ride tomorrow?"

Banner ran a hand down her face in a fit of frustration. "Who told you I wasn't?"

"Your foreman mentioned it at dinner. You don't eat with your guests, you don't go on the trail rides, but you call yourself our hostess. Interesting." His dark eyes glittered and he pursed his lips slightly as if he were fighting off a grin.

"I usually go along on the trail rides," she corrected him. "I might go tomorrow. I haven't made up my mind." Forcing herself to calm down, she faced him with what she hoped was the essence of tolerance. "Did you come here to register a complaint about my role here? My staff is small but efficient. Pete Parker can handle the trail rides without me."

He propped his elbows on his bent knees and leaned closer. "You don't like me, do you?"

Banner took a few moments to size up her adversary. There was a brooding cast to his face, enhanced by his full lower lip and heavy, dark brows. Dark stubble shadowed the lower half of his face. There was a latent sexuality about him, Banner decided. It lurked just beneath the surface of his half smile, and Banner had the feeling that it wouldn't take much for it to emerge, full-blown and potent.

"You've done everything possible to get my dander up since you came in here," she noted. "It seems to me that you don't want me to like you."

"On the contrary," he said, his voice as smooth as glass. "I want very much for you to like me. I sense that you're uncomfortable around me. Is it because I was born Russian?"

"Don't be silly," she scoffed, but heard the flighty, breathless lie in her voice. "I don't care where you were born or raised or where you live now."

"I live in Houston in a condo."

"Good for you," she said, glaring at him for interrupting. Did he actually think she wanted to know where he lived? "Mr. Mytova, I'm very busy. If you came in here to hurl insults and needle me then I'd appreciate it—"

"What happened to 'Yuri'?" His dark brows lowered in a scowl. "I thought we were on a first-name basis around here."

She hated him for throwing her earlier words back in her face. "Yuri, I'm busy!" She swallowed the hysterical note in her voice. "If you've got a legitimate beef, let's hear it. If not, let me see you to the door." She stood up and stared down at him.

"Legitimate beef," he said, smiling. "Where do Americans come up with such language?"

"It's *my* language and I'm proud of it!" Her patience snapped like a dry twig and, too late, she realized that she was leaning over the desk and glaring at him, her hands gathered into tight fists of rage.

He stood up and thrust his face close to hers. "My language, too, Banner. And I, too, am proud of it." A grin overtook him, then a short laugh of delight. "Shall we raise our voices in a chorus of 'America the Beautiful'?"

She felt her face flush with embarrassment. "You're rude and obnoxious," she said, then wished she'd kept her thoughts to herself. She'd unwittingly conceded to him. He'd come in here to hear her confess her dislike for him and she'd done it!

He accepted her insult with a slight nod of his head. "And you're a beautiful woman, Banner O'Bryan."

She closed her eyes and sighed wearily. He was impossible, impudent and imperious. He was also much too close for comfort. She leaned back from him, feeling her nerve ends flutter. Might as well concede the other point, she thought. If she was going to lose, she might as well lose everything.

"I'll go on the trail ride in the morning," she said in a toneless voice, hoping that he would leave now that he had his pound of flesh.

It worked like a charm. Yuri backed off, smiled a friendly, less predatory smile, and started for the door.

"Wonderful, wonderful," he murmured, then turned back to her as he opened the office door. "We're going to get along fine, aren't we? By the end of my two weeks' stay I'll wager that we'll be good friends."

Banner tipped up her chin, insulted by his placating air. "I wouldn't bet on it. Close the door on your way out, please."

His low, throaty chuckle floated to her before the door sealed it off.

Banner dropped like a stone into the chair and rested her forehead on her crossed arms.

"I hate him," she whispered through gritted teeth. "Overbearing, arrogant..." She raised her head and glared at the door. "Communist!"

But he wasn't, she corrected herself. We wouldn't have allowed him in America if he were a "party" man. Why did we let him in? she wondered. Did he defect or did the Soviets trade him for someone more desirable? Must have been a trade, she decided with a twist of malice. America's loss, Russia's gain.

Two

"What made you decide to come on the trail ride?" Pete asked as he reined his horse beside Banner's.

Banner dismounted, watched the two ranch hands help the guests from their horses, then began leading her palomino to the stables. "Who could stay inside on such a pretty morning?"

"I agree with you there," Pete said, guiding his pinto into the stall beside Banner's horse. "I always love the first rides when the tenderfoots have to get used to their horses and toughen up their backsides." Pete chuckled and began loosening his mount's saddle. "And there's always a surprise or two. Take that Russian fella..."

"Yuri," Banner supplied, tired of hearing him referred to as "that Russian fella" by her staff. "His name is Yuri. What about him?"

"I figured he'd be as comfortable on a horse as a fly on a

hot skillet, but he's a natural! Rode that horse like he was born to the saddle. Didn't you notice?"

Notice? How could she not notice since Yuri insisted on riding beside her or right behind her throughout the entire trail ride? Eluding him had been about as easy as eluding her shadow.

She nodded absently to Pete's question and began unsaddling Honey. The morning had started with a surprise: Yuri Mytova in snug jeans, a black Western-cut shirt and boots. In an unguarded moment she'd smiled, and Yuri had seen her pleased expression. He'd hooked his thumbs in his belt and tossed her a questioning smile as if to say, "What do you think?"

He'd laughed when she'd whirled away from the sight of him.

"Oooo, that man!"

"What man?" Pete asked, peeking over the back of his horse at her.

"What?" Banner stared vacantly at him, realizing only then that she'd spoken aloud. "Oh, nothing."

Pete crossed his arms on the pinto's back and studied Banner carefully. "What's going on with you? You've been out of sorts all winter. I thought you'd snap out of it when the ranch opened again, but you're still...well, preoccupied. And don't tell me it's spring fever."

Banner shrugged off his persistent questioning. He was right, of course. She'd been restless of late, but she hadn't a clue as to why. She loved the ranch and the people on it, but she didn't like the routine. Funny that she hadn't thought of her work as routine while her father had been alive, she mused as she brushed Honey's damp coat. Lucas had made everything fun for her. She'd been his princess, coddled, catered to, and, yes, spoiled. Lucas had spoiled her, but why not? They had weathered the desertion of her mother together and emerged stronger and more devoted to each other than ever before.

Her thoughts returned to her twenty-first birthday. She remembered the melancholy look in her father's eyes that day.

"What's wrong, Dad?" she'd asked.

"Oh, I was just thinking that you're a grown woman now—a lovely woman. Someday a handsome man will take you away from here. I'll miss you, hon. The place won't be the same without you."

"I'm not going anywhere," she'd vowed, sensing that Luke was preparing himself for her departure. "I won't leave you. I'll never leave you. I love the ranch. It's my home and it always will be."

I'm not like Mother, she'd thought, knowing that her father was thinking the same thing. I won't desert you. I won't break your heart like she did.

She replaced the brush on its shelf and turned, then gasped softly when she found herself inches from Yuri Mytova.

"Would you like to join me for a drink at the saloon?" he asked, propping one hand high up on the wall.

"No, thanks." She glanced over at the other stall. "Where's Pete?"

"Gone." Yuri grinned and dipped his head so that his face was close to hers. "We're all alone." His heavy brows moved up and down, accentuating his hushed tone. "I've got you cornered. You're at my mercy."

"I'm not amused," Banner said, pressing a hand against his chest and giving him a good shove. "Excuse me."

"Are you always this rude to your guests?" he asked, grabbing one of her wrists before she could get past him.

"Rude?" She stared at him incredulously. "*You're* calling *me* rude? Incredible!" She jerked her arm, but his fingers tightened around her wrist. "Let go of me. This isn't funny."

"And I'm not laughing." With an economy of movement, he turned her around and pushed her back against the rough wall. His hands moved up to her shoulders. "What have you got against me? Why do you run every time you see me?"

"I'm not running," she argued. "I have better things to do than play stupid cat-and-mouse games with you."

"Do you?" His hands drifted down her arms, lightly caressed her trembling fingers and were gone. "Go ahead. No one's stopping you. Why aren't you moving, Banner? What's holding you in place?"

What was holding her in place was the earthy color of his eyes—dark, chocolate brown, almost black. The danger of him appealed to the streak of recklessness within her. She was imprisoned by her own overwhelming need to break free of routine, to taste forbidden fruit, to shatter the predictability of her world. She felt like a rabbit blinded by headlights, sensing the fear but held in place by a fascination for the unknown.

He was offering her an escape, but she couldn't make herself move. Even as he dipped his head lower, she stood motionless. His mouth touched hers lightly, questioningly.

"Now's your chance," he whispered. "You'd better run while there's still time."

She didn't move a muscle other than to close her eyes.

He tasted her lips again and again, soft, sipping kisses that made her head swim. His fingers eased through the sides of her hair, holding her head in place as his mouth covered hers.

He tasted of dark, rich things: imported caviar, chocolate bonbons, intoxicating Black Russians.

She tasted of light, clean things: mountain springs, babbling brooks, crystalline raindrops.

His body pressed against hers, and Banner let her hands slip down his body to his thighs, then around to his tightly muscled hips. He was solid, she thought. Something to hold on to, someone to lean on.

His lips moved across her cheek, down her throat, across her collarbone. Banner drew a quivering breath before his mouth claimed hers again, no longer sipping, but drinking her in.

What are you doing? Logic screamed in her ear, breaking through her lethargy and snapping her out of her self-induced trance. It gave her strength, and she shoved Yuri away and stumbled out of his embrace. She pressed her hands to her cheeks, feeling her hot skin and recognizing the heat of passion. Horrified, she stared at him and shook her head as if to deny what had happened.

His smile was at once apologetic and triumphant.

"It's too late to run now," he murmured. "The deed is done."

"Stay away from me," she said, suddenly afraid of him. "Do you hear me? You stay away from me!"

He shook his head slowly from side to side. "Too late for that, Banner O'Bryan. In Russia it is said that every kiss leaves an imprint on the heart. I'm imprinted on you."

"That's ridiculous," she said, backing away from him.

"Do you believe in fate... in destiny?"

"No!" She clamped her hands over her ears for a moment, her eyes wide; then she whirled and ran from the stables.

"I do," he whispered after her. "I do."

Banner ran headlong through the house and to her quarters. She locked the double doors behind her and hurried through the office to the living room. She sat on the oyster-colored couch and hid her face in her hands, ashamed of her conduct. Moaning, she wondered how in the world she could face Yuri again. He'd laugh at her. He'd taunt her. He'd humiliate her.

Her mind scrambled for a solution. She'd leave. She'd just pack some things and go somewhere—Fort Gibson, Tahlequah, Tulsa. Anywhere but here! She'd run—

"No." Pride surged through her, dividing her shame, and she sat up straight. "I will not run away from him. This is my home. *My* home. I won't let him drive me out of it!"

She stood up and paced the length of the living room while she gathered her defenses. She'd ignore him. She wouldn't take his bait. She'd act as if nothing had happened. After all, it was just a few kisses. Nothing to get worked up about.

Her thoughts mocked her. She *had* gotten worked up over his kisses. There was something about him, something predatory and savage. She felt as if she were his prey. Danger sizzled around him, drawing and repelling her at the same time.

Perhaps she was mildly flattered that he wanted her so openly. He'd made no bones about it. It was the first time a man had doggedly pursued her, and it was natural that she might be titillated by that, she reasoned. Pursuit was exciting, especially when she was being chased by such an attractive man. Why had he decided to pursue her? It wasn't love at first sight or anything that high-minded. Lust was more like it, Banner thought with a wry smile. Had he come here looking for an easy roll in the hay? Was it that simple... that disgusting?

No, it was more than that. A man as attractive as Yuri Mytova didn't have to come to a dude ranch in Oklahoma to procure a woman. He could have stayed in Houston for that! Any number of women would be more than happy to—

Banner's thoughts slid to an abrupt halt when she found herself gazing at one of her mother's paintings above the mantel. It was a watercolor depiction of the ranch and the sight of it reminded Banner of just what type of woman found pushy Russians irresistible.

"I'm not like you," she said in a vicious whisper. "I'm not looking to being swept off my feet and carried off to some big city by a foreigner!"

She went to the mantel and gripped the edge of it until her knuckles showed white under her skin. Staring up at the painting, she tried to see it for what it was—an early work by a highly touted American artist—but all she could see was flowing colors that signified nothing. Just like her mother. All flash and little substance. The last communication she'd had with her mother had been on her sixteenth birthday. Diana had called her long distance from New York, and Banner had been filled with adolescent self-righteousness.

"You hate me, don't you?" Diana had asked after suffering through a few minutes of Banner's monosyllabic answers to her questions.

"Yes," Banner had replied haughtily.

"Well, you have just cause," Diana had said, and her voice hadn't been sad, but only resigned. "I won't bother you again because I know you don't want to hear from me. I just wanted to wish you a happy birthday and a good life. Someday, when you're older and you fall desperately in love with a man, I hope you'll understand why I did what I did."

"Which man are you talking about?" Banner had asked.

"I loved your father, Banner, but not enough. Luke is a good man—"

"I know," Banner had interrupted, anxious for this conversation to end. "Dad's a wonderful man."

"Yes, but he's not the right man for me."

"I have to go. Dad's giving me a birthday party."

"Okay, I won't keep you. Banner?"

"Yes?"

"I love you, darling. You don't have to love me back. That's not necessary. I just want you to know that I love you and will always love you. Be happy, sweetheart."

"I am happy, no thanks to you!" Banner had slammed down the receiver and fought back bitter tears.

Looking up at the painting again, Banner's eyes filled with the tears she'd denied ten years ago.

"I'm older, Diana," she said to the painting, "but I still don't understand how you could turn your back on Dad and me. There's no excuse for what you did to us. Dad forgave you, but I won't!"

When she'd received the news of her mother's death she had been almost as relieved as if a dark cloud had lifted from her life and from her father's life. Diana had provided for Banner in her will, but Banner had refused to touch one cent. She'd donated the money to charity, even though her father had urged her to put it in savings.

Banner had wanted to sell the painting, too, but Luke had insisted on keeping it.

"It's all we have left of her," he'd said in a choked voice. "I can't part with it. I don't want you to sell it—ever!"

Banner turned her back on the painting and wondered how her father could have loved her mother to the bitter end. Diana had died along with Vladimir Zaarbo in an automobile accident on California's Pacific Coast Highway. Luke had mourned her passing as if she were still his wife. Banner had witnessed his grief with a mixture of pity and anger. She felt sorry for him, but she also wanted to berate him for loving a woman who had scorned him years ago.

Well, no matter, Banner thought. Diana had hurt Luke, but Banner had done the right thing. Banner had stayed with her father and loved the land as passionately as Luke had loved it.

She had done the right thing, and she would continue to do the right thing. Tomorrow she would face Yuri Mytova squarely. She wouldn't be intimidated by him. She wouldn't run away. She would stand her ground and, in less than two weeks, he'd be gone and she could slip back into her comfortable, secure routine.

As it turned out, Banner had nothing to worry about. Over the next two days, Yuri Mytova kept his distance from her as if he, too, was embarrassed over the incident in the stables. Short trail rides were scheduled each day and Yuri went along, almost grudgingly.

Since he kept his distance, Banner was given the opportunity to observe him. She decided that he was a loner and usually preoccupied with his private thoughts. When the riders stopped for lunch and gathered into a big circle around the chuck wagon, Yuri wandered off to sit beneath a tree and covet his own company. When the other guests gathered at the Shortbranch in the evenings, Banner noticed that Yuri stayed in his cabin.

Although Banner was grateful that Yuri's attraction to her had waned, her nerves were stretched tight. She kept expecting him to approach her...no, ambush would be a better word, she thought as she left the shadows of the stable and stepped into the bright sunlight in the corral.

At least Yuri wasn't any trouble on the trail rides. He rode with a lanky ease, always confident and controlled. Several of the other guests were first-timers, and Banner and Pete kept wary eyes on them as they jostled in the saddle and tugged fitfully at the reins. Teaching tenderfoots how to ride was part of the dude ranch business. Keeping them safe was uppermost in Banner's mind. The trail horses were used to nervous riders, but horses were as unpredictable as people, and Banner and Pete spent a good deal of their time issuing instructions to the novice riders.

However, Yuri didn't need instructions. Pete had given him one of the more spirited horses to ride, a chestnut called

Rusty. Banner smiled at herself, remembering how high-strung she'd been the other day when she'd waited for Yuri to tease her or make some reference to their earlier encounter, but he'd acted as if nothing had happened. That had been *her* plan of action—to ignore him—but he'd stolen her thunder.

Standing in the center of the corral with the sun warming her skin, Banner closed her eyes and saw him as he'd looked earlier today astride Rusty. The morning light had picked out the silver strands in his sideburns and, once, she thought she'd seen a strand or two of silver in the dark hair that swept across his forehead. He had a regal nose, proud and straight with nostrils that flared slightly. His jawline was square with a stamp of determination. She had noticed the extremities of his nature in the way his eyes softened when he talked with precocious Fawn Ferguson, only to darken to a dangerous, pitchy color when one of the other guests had blurted out, "It's a damned pity what the Russians are doing in Afghanistan. Americans don't cotton to folks who barge into a country and try to take over."

"Oh, no?" Yuri had said in a deceptively soft voice. "I believe the native American Indians would disagree with you."

The others had laughed nervously, and the subject had been dropped abruptly. At times, he wasn't such an ogre, she conceded. She admired the way he handled himself. Did he miss Russia? Did he feel like an American or an expatriate?

Suddenly she shivered and looked around warily. She felt as if she were being watched, but no one was in sight. Shaking off the eerie feeling, Banner snapped out of her reverie and went toward the house.

Yuri stepped from the shadows of the stables as Banner disappeared inside the house. He lit a cigarette and leaned lazily against a rough post, enjoying the cigarette and his feelings toward Banner.

She was a paper tiger, he decided—growling and ferocious, but frail and frightened of anything unfamiliar. He frightened her. He'd seen that the other day in the stables when she'd become completely unhinged, simply because she'd accepted his advances.

Yuri ground the cigarette into the dirt with his boot and headed in the direction of his cabin. Of course, she hadn't been the only one who'd become unhinged, he taunted himself. He'd lost control, too. He had meant to test the waters... one little kiss just to see how she reacted. But she was like candy. One taste wasn't enough. One taste just whetted his appetite and he'd wanted more... he'd wanted all of her.

He couldn't remember the last time he'd wanted a woman so badly. Must have been back in Moscow, he thought, but he couldn't pinpoint the woman or the moment. The way his senses had surged when he'd kissed her had alarmed him and made him retreat into a shell. He needed time to sort through his feelings and be true to himself. He wasn't the type to fool himself or to "go with the flow," as his fellow Americans said. No, he had to know who and why and when and how much. He was an engineer. He dealt with facts, not hunches.

So to what or whom had he reacted that day in the stables? he wondered as he entered his cabin. To Diana's memory or Banner's reality?

His father had written so vibrantly, so passionately of Diana that any red-blooded male would have fallen in love with her right along with Vladimir. Loving Diana through Vladimir had been safe, and Yuri had been seeking safety at the time. He'd lived through a period of trauma and heart-thumping fear during his defection and, once he'd been granted diplomatic immunity in America, he'd sought security and asylum. He'd wanted a quiet life of dedication, and he'd lived like a monk in his Houston condo. No women. No recreation. No surprises. Work was his hiding place, his sole purpose, his peace of mind.

He needed it now, he thought, drawn to books and blueprints strewn across the coffee table. He sat on the floor and slipped on a pair of reading glasses—his first purchase as an American. The glasses he'd worn in Russia were best described as blatantly unattractive. His eyes had nearly popped out when he'd seen the array of frames shown to him during his visit to a Houston optometrist. He'd selected gray frames with smoky lenses, a far cry from the black-framed, clunky pair he'd worn in Moscow.

Flipping through a book, he settled more comfortably on the floor. His supervisor wouldn't have approved if he'd known that Yuri had taken work along on his vacation. All work and no play and all that rot. But this wasn't classified information. Yuri picked up another heavy volume and opened it, remembering the vast Houston libraries he loved so dearly where he'd found these books and blueprints. There was so much to learn about American aeronautics and he was an overeager student.

He started reading, then smiled when he realized that he was reading and comprehending in English instead of reading English and mentally translating into Russian. The mark of true fluency, he thought with pride. English was quickly becoming his primary language.

An hour later he realized that his cross-legged position on the floor had kinked his overtaxed muscles. He stood up, groaning when his back and shoulder muscles tightened. Damn horses, he thought with a grimace. He hadn't ridden since he was a teenager, and his muscles reminded him of that as he kneaded the small of his back and moved stiffly across the room and out onto the porch. He bent at the waist, seeking relief, and swayed from side to side to lengthen the bunched muscles. His vertebrae popped, a muscle in his back contracted painfully and his breath whistled noisily down his windpipe.

He cursed viciously, calling up a few of the more colorfully explicit words he'd learned from some of the enlisted men at NASA, then flung back his head and shut his eyes tightly as he waited for the sharp pain to lessen.

"Are you okay?"

His eyes flew open and his heart skipped a beat when he saw Banner, standing only a few feet from him. She was looking up at him, a look of concern on her lovely face. Did she have any idea of how beautiful she was?

"I'm...f-fine," he stuttered, then straightened and struggled for equilibrium. "Just a little sore, that's all."

She tucked her hands into her back pockets and looked up at him through her thick lashes. "Where did you learn language like that? You cuss like a sailor!"

"No, like an aviator," he said, grinning. "Those fly boys love the color blue."

"Oh, I see." She laughed softly and stared at the ground for a few moments in silence, wondering if she should leave him alone. Go, while the going's good, she told herself, but something in the way he smiled at her overruled the logic. He had a nice smile, she thought, glancing at him, then quickly away. Most of the time he had smirked at her, but he was smiling this time—a tender, trustworthy smile.

"Where did you learn to ride?" she asked, hoping he'd stay friendly and not resort to his usual arrogance.

He seemed to think about her question for a moment before he answered, "My grandparents lived in the country. They had a couple of farm horses and they let me ride them when I visited. Both horses were big and strong, and it took every ounce of my strength to control them, but I liked the challenge. I like being in control."

"Do you have other family in Russia? A wife, perhaps?" She wished she could have taken back the last part of the question when his smile faded.

"I wouldn't have kissed you if I had a wife waiting back in Moscow," he said with deadly earnest. "I have family in Russia, but no wife or children."

"I'm sorry if I offended you," she said, shrugging off his stinging words. "But you wouldn't be the first man to have an adulterous fling. A lot of men operate under the adage, Out of Sight, Out of Mind."

"Not this man."

She regarded his stern expression and decided he was telling the truth. "Are you enjoying your vacation?"

"I suppose." He leaned a shoulder against the porch railing and crossed his arms against his chest. "I'd rather be working."

"Why?"

He shook his head, baffled by her lack of comprehension. "Why?" he echoed. "Because when I'm working, I'm accomplishing. I accomplish nothing by being idle."

"Relaxation's important. Everyone needs to kick back and charge the batteries."

He grinned, amused by her figure of speech. "My battery is charged by my work. What gets you all charged up?"

She was instantly on guard, but she struggled not to show it. "This place," she said, sweeping one arm to encompass the grassy area around her. "I get my strength from this land."

"Just like Scarlett O'Hara," he mocked and his smirk was back in place. "The red earth of Rocking Horse gives you strength, does it?"

"That's right," she said, tipping up her chin in a defiant angle. "I love this place!"

"Okay, okay!" He held up his hands in surrender. "Are you trying to convince me or yourself?"

She glowered at him, then decided not to dignify his question with an answer. "I was on my way to the town. You'll excuse me."

He studied her straight back, the haughty tilt of her chin, her brisk stride. Queenly, he thought. Had she been daddy's little princess?

"Did your mother love this place with the same passion?"

She whirled, her eyes wide, her mouth slightly opened by surprise. "Why do you ask about my mother?" Her tone was sharp, speaking fathoms.

Yuri examined her flushed face and felt sorry for her. "No particular reason," he lied. "I assumed you had one."

"I... yes." She swallowed hard and looked away from him. "My parents were... I'm from a broken home."

Broken home. What an odd way to put it, Yuri thought. She reminded him of that paper tiger again. Tough and tender. Brave and trembling.

"So am I," he said, wanting to heal the wound he'd callously opened.

"You are?"

"Yes. My father... left us when I was fourteen."

"My mother left for good when I was ten."

"For good?"

She chewed on her lower lip for a few moments, then kicked at a patch of wildflowers. "She wasn't here much. She was an artist, and she was always on trips to New York and places like that. She never liked it here." A bitter frown twisted her mouth. "She was always looking for beautiful things to paint, but she was so shortsighted that she never realized that this is the most beautiful place on earth."

"You've been all over the earth?" he challenged.

"No, but I've been around," she said defensively.

"Where?"

"Fort Gibson, Tulsa, Tahlequah. I went to school for a while in Oklahoma City."

"It sounds to me as if you've reduced the earth to the size of Oklahoma," he said with a lazy smile. "You Sooners don't have a monopoly on beautiful places, you know." He gazed over her head at a distant point. "There's a big, wide world out there, Banner. Perhaps your mother wanted to see more of it than her own backyard afforded."

"You don't know what you're talking about." She turned her back on him. "My mother was irresponsible and self-centered. She didn't care about anyone but herself!"

"You don't think she cared about you?"

She laughed mirthlessly. "She never gave me a second thought. I've got to go." She started forward, but paused to glance over her shoulder at him. "Her name was Diana Dufrayne. Have you heard of her?"

"I believe so," he hedged, hating himself for his own deceit. He should tell her his real name, but he was afraid. They were both paper tigers.

"She was pretty famous, I guess. Her paintings are in most of the major galleries."

"Do you have artistic talents?"

"No." She seemed offended by the suggestion. "I take after my father."

Yuri watched as she made her way along the path toward the small tourist town, then he turned and went back into his cabin. Poor misguided Banner, he thought with a twinge of pity. She was determined to paint her mother in dark, foreboding colors, but he knew better. Diana had been a woman of blinding boldness. Reds, blues, yellows, greens. Primary colors of rainbow brightness.

He went to the window and drew back one panel of the draperies. He could see the path through the trees and he caught a glimpse of Banner's pink shirt.

"She thought of you, Banner," he whispered in Diana's defense. "You were always on her mind." He leaned his forehead against the cool glass and closed his eyes. "And, lately, you're always on *my* mind." He shuddered to think about what that meant and where it might lead him.

Three

The campfire crackled and spit, uncommonly loud now that the other guests had wandered off to their cabins after an evening of roasting marshmallows. Pete and Cookie put aside their guitars, ending the evening's serenade of country and Western standards that had reminded Yuri of Russian folk songs.

Yuri watched Banner through the smoke and flames as she bid good-night to Pete and Cookie. Dressed in tight jeans and a bulky gray sweater, she looked cuddly and warm. She had held his attention all evening, proving to be a fascinating subject. He liked the way she treated her guests, speaking to each one during the evening. She was friendly, but not overly so. She'd even spoken to him briefly, urging him to taste the roasted marshmallows. Her speech inflections were lovely, a soft, easy drawl that was different from the Texas accents he'd grown used to.

The night grew quiet once Pete and Cookie had left, and Banner looked around, spotted Yuri and swallowed hard. Wasn't he going to leave like the others? she wondered, smiling timidly at him. She squared her shoulders and walked around the campfire to him, since there was no graceful way to avoid him.

"Is the party over?" he asked.

"Looks that way," she replied, stopping beside him. She smiled nervously, wondering what to do next...what to say to him. She'd never been at a loss for words with her guests, but she couldn't converse with him. Every time she talked with him she said things she regretted.

"I suppose you're waiting for me to leave so that you can go into the house," he said, then tipped back his head and gazed at the stars. "You go on. I'm not ready to go to my cabin yet. I want to stay here a few minutes longer and commune with the heavens."

"You enjoy being alone, don't you?"

"Sometimes." But not right now, he thought. Right now I wish you'd sit beside me and quit treating me as if I were a wild, ferocious animal. He patted the ground beside him, but kept his gaze on the starry sky. "Sit down. You don't have to be afraid of me."

"I'm not afraid of you."

He smiled and angled his head sideways. "Then sit down and prove it."

She hesitated long enough to note the tightness of his jawline and the tension that seemed to radiate from him. He sat perfectly still, his knees bent and his arms looped around them, but she sensed that he was wound as tight as a pocket watch. Banner kept the smile from her lips as she sat next to him and was pleased when he released a long sigh of satisfaction. It was comforting to know that he was as uneasy around her as she was around him.

Glancing at him from the corner of her eye, she felt the irresistible pull of him. He acted like a magnet on her, tugging and drawing her closer even as she tried to break the contact. He baffled her and her reaction to him was confusing. Why was she drawn to him? He'd been obnoxious, arrogant and rude to her, but there was something about him that made her want to know him, to read his mind, to become lost in him.

"Banner," he said suddenly, making her snap to attention. "Where did you get that delightful name?"

"When I was born my mother said it was a banner day." She laughed softly as memories of her younger days when her mother and father had been together engulfed her.

"Banner bright," Yuri murmured.

Banner gasped softly, her eyes widening in alarm as she turned sideways to face him. "Wh-what did you say?"

He wished he could take back the slip of his tongue. "Banner bright," he repeated, watching as trepidation darkened her eyes. "Why are you looking at me like that? It's just an expression." But he knew why she was looking at him that way. He'd read that description in his father's diary. Diana had referred to her daughter as Banner Bright.

"N-nothing," Banner stuttered, looking away from him and hunching her shoulders in a protective way. "It's just that... my mother used to call me that."

"I'm sorry. I didn't mean to dredge up bad memories." He sighed, feeling like a coward. He should tell her about his connection to her, he told himself, but couldn't make himself speak the words. "I have bad memories, too."

"How did you get out of Russia? Did they just let you go or were you traded for someone?"

He smiled, amused by her innocence. "Traded? Like a baseball player from one team to another?" He chuckled and removed the black cowboy hat from his head, then combed his fingers through his straight dark hair. "No, it wasn't that easy. I was smuggled out."

"Smuggled?" She turned around, curling her legs to one side and giving him her full attention. "Like contraband? That sounds exciting. I suppose it was dangerous, too."

"It was both," he agreed. "And it was terrifying. I wouldn't want to go through it again."

"So you escaped," she said, piecing it together. "They didn't want to let you go."

"That's right. I worked for the space program. They don't let people like me go to America just for the asking."

"How were you smuggled? By plane?"

"No, in a cargo ship." Those black horrible hours reached back for him with sticky fingers. He leaned back from the fire, no longer needing its warmth now that he'd broken out in a sweat. "I risked everything to come here and now I must make it worthwhile." Thoughts of the ship...the darkness always suffocated him. He gathered a deep breath to clear his head. "I have to make a success of my life," he explained, but he could tell by her expression that she didn't quite understand. How could she? There was so much she didn't know about sacrifice. "I not only endangered myself but my entire family, and I love my family very much. You understand?"

She nodded, touched by his heartfelt expression of love.

"I'll probably never see them again." He ran his hand through his hair, then rested his chin on his crossed arms and stared moodily at the fire's final glow. "That hurts."

"Oh, Yuri," she whispered, laying a slender hand on his sleeve. "You miss them, don't you?"

"Yes." He swallowed the lump of emotion that had wedged in his throat. "So it's important for me to be successful here. I gave up everything for my freedom."

"You're already successful. You're working for NASA."

He shrugged off the compliment. "I have a lot to learn. I'm working on a space station now. Someday Americans will be traveling to outposts in space just as they used to travel to forts in this area. I want to make that happen. I want to be part of America's history—one of her favorite stepsons."

The fervency in his voice startled her. He was so determined, she thought. So intense.

"What do you want to do with your life, Banner?"

She shrugged, wondering where to begin, then realized that her goals were childishly simple. What could she do here besides keep things running on their usual course?

"I guess I'm doing it," she answered lamely, feeling that restlessness move through her like wind through a willow.

"This is it? This is all you want?" he asked, sweeping a hand to encompass the darkness outside the glow of embers.

"This happens to be prime property," she said, defensive again. "I guess you'd rather see condos built on it."

"No, I just assumed you had more lofty goals than to simply live day-to-day."

"I do!" Her voice rose with agitation.

"Then what are they?"

She was silent for a few moments, trying to think of something that would appease him. "There's room for improvement here."

"That's certainly true."

Her gaze was sharp and cutting. "I'm not talking about adding room service!"

"What, then?"

"More activities, maybe a restaurant."

"I can tell you've given this a lot of thought," he said with dry sarcasm.

"I'm not out to make the history books," she returned with her own measure of sarcasm. "I just want to lead a good and honest life."

"Don't you ever want to leave this place?"

"No. I have responsibilities here."

"But you could keep this place running and still pursue other dreams that have nothing to do with the ranch."

"Dreams." She smiled sadly, then stood up and used a small branch to sweep the embers into a wider circle until they were nothing but ashes. "You have to be careful of dreams. They can swindle you in your sleep."

Yuri smiled, thinking over what she'd said. "You don't dream?"

"Not anymore. I used to when I was a kid, but I've discovered that dreams make promises they can't keep."

"You sound disillusioned, Banner."

"Maybe I am." She looked up at the stars, letting the branch fall from her fingers. "Maybe that's what's been bothering me."

"So, you aren't completely satisfied," he noted, smiling when she appeared startled. "You just admitted it, didn't you?"

She shrugged. "It's nothing. Just a phase." She brushed her hands together briskly and sighed. "I'm going inside. It's chilly."

"Sit by me and I'll warm you up."

Banner regarded him carefully: his shining eyes, his wide mouth, his straight black hair. So handsome, she thought. He could have any woman. "Why are you picking on me?"

He arched one dark brow. "You don't know?"

"No, I don't. Tell me."

"I thought I'd made my intentions clear to you the other day in the stables. I'm picking on you—as you put it—because you're beautiful and I want to get to know you."

"Get to know me?" she repeated with a lilt. "Don't you mean you want to go to bed with me?"

He grinned wickedly. "You see? You *do* know why I've been picking on you."

She laughed softly, shaking her head as if she didn't believe him. "Sorry, but I'm not interested. Besides, I'm sure that you have plenty of women friends in Houston."

"I stumble over them at every turn," he wisecracked. "How perceptive of you to notice."

"I didn't." She looked away, barely able to keep the smile from her lips. "Why did you come here? You don't like riding or roping or square dancing. Why did you pick this place?"

"Maybe I knew you'd be here."

She wrinkled her nose playfully. "No, seriously. Why did you come here?"

"To vacation, of course." He rose lazily to his feet and stretched.

"But why did you pick a dude ranch?"

"Because it's so...American. I never played cowboys and Indians when I was a child. I thought I might have missed out on something important."

"We don't play cowboys and Indians here," she objected good-naturedly. "You're not having fun, are you? You wish you were in Houston."

"I wish I was at work," he granted, "but I'm having fun right now."

"You are?" She studied him carefully, minutely. "It's hard to tell. You never seem to be having a good time. You're...serious-natured. Too serious, I think."

"In other words, I'm a stick-in-the-mud. Boring. Unimaginative. Not your cup of tea. Dull as dishwater. A cure for insomnia."

She laughed as he piled one cliché on top of the other. "You're not that bad! What do you do in Houston on Friday nights?"

"I read." He laughed when she sighed and rolled her eyes. "You've got something against literacy?"

"No, but it's not a party, is it? What do you do on Saturday nights?"

"Same thing."

"Oh, Yuri, come on! You have women friends, don't you? You do date, right?"

"Not recently." The conversation became maudlin for him, making him too aware of his solitary existence of late.

"What about those women you've been stumbling over?"

"What about you?" he asked, turning the tables on her. "What do you do on Friday and Saturday nights? Who are you dating?"

"Well, I've got to work," she said, excusing herself. "I have guests to see to and—"

"No personal life? No love life?"

"I didn't say that."

"So, what's his name?"

"There isn't anyone right now," she said testily. "Okay? Are you satisfied?"

"Are you?"

His soft, consoling voice brought her gaze to his again, and she felt a bond forming between them.

"I'm not," he said, reaching out a hand and trailing his fingertips down her cheek. "You are the most exquisite thing," he whispered as his gaze lingered on her mouth. "You ask me why I've decided to pursue you, and I can only ask how could I keep from it? How could any man look at you and not want you?"

"Yuri, don't." She turned her head and color rose in her cheeks. "Let's keep it friendly."

"Yes. Close, intimate friends." He curled his hand under her chin and brought her face around to his. "You like me, don't you?"

"In a weird way, yes." She smiled, trying to get him in a playful mood.

"You want me to kiss you, don't you?"

"No, I don't want that." She stiffened and tried to pull her chin from his hand, but his fingers tightened. "You . . . you frighten me when you're like this."

"Frighten you?" He shook his head slowly and starlight reflected in his eyes. "No, Banner. You're confusing fear with desire. I've known both. Both make your heart beat faster and both make you squirm with indecision, but fear demoralizes and desire exhilarates. That's the difference." He touched his lips to hers, then drew away. "We could be good for each other."

"I'm sorry, Yuri, but I'm not convinced of that." She backed away from him, almost reluctantly. "I'm going inside. Good night."

Yuri waited until she'd closed the door before he reached down and retrieved his hat from the ground. Brushing grass from it, he wondered if he shouldn't confess to Banner that they shared a common thread. He had meant to meet her, quench his curiosity and leave without her ever knowing that he was Vladimir's son, but things were getting out of hand. He wanted her trust, but he knew he'd have to earn it. He'd have to tell her. He couldn't let this deception stand between them.

But when and how? He stared up at the stars, bright and countless. Banner Bright. How could he have imagined what an impact she'd have on him? He wanted her; he wanted her so much that even now he ached to hold her.

"Ah, Banner," he whispered to the twinkling stars. "We're on a collision course, you and I, and neither of us will escape without injury."

Yuri waited impatiently for his supervisor at NASA to pick up the phone. The operator cut in, informing Yuri of additional charges, and he slipped three more coins into the pay phone.

"Hello, Jeff Peterson here."

"Jeff, it's Yuri."

"Hey, partner! What's happening?"

"I just called to ask about the project. Did those cost projections come in?"

"Yuri, Yuri, Yuri," Jeff chanted indulgently. "What am I going to do with you? You're on vacation, buddy. What the hell do you care if the projections came in or not? Kick up your heels and enjoy yourself!"

"Did they come in?" Yuri asked with a sigh of irritation.

"Yes. Everything's 'go'. We got the funding, we got the green light and we're forging ahead. How's the dude ranch? Have you roped any dogies yet?"

"No." Yuri turned around to watch some of the guests try their skills at tossing horseshoes. "I'm glad to hear that things are going smoothly there. I'm anxious to get back to Houston... back to my work."

"You know what you need, partner?"

"What?" Yuri asked with a labored sigh because he knew what was coming. Jeff's cure for everything was sex.

"You need to find you a pretty little Oklahoma gal and a big old haystack. Some hanky-panky will fix you up, bud. There's nothing like it. Hell, I'm getting worked up just thinking about it!"

"What about the launch?" Yuri asked, his voice dripping with irritation. "Is it still scheduled for Friday?"

"The launch? I'm talking about women and all you can think about is setting off a rocket? Man, oh, man! You're in dire straits, pal."

"Is the launch on schedule, Jeff?"

"Yes, Yuri." Jeff sighed with exaggeration. "Now about finding a woman in a haystack..."

"Goodbye, Jeff." Yuri whirled, slammed the phone into its cradle and closed his eyes in frustration. "Trying to talk to you is like trying to talk to an oversexed teenager!"

"Pardon?"

Yuri opened his eyes to Banner's mischievous grin. He laughed softly, realizing she'd overheard his last denouncement. "I was talking about my boss. I just called to check in on how things are going at NASA."

Banner leaned against the outside wall of the main house and pushed her lower lip into a pretty pout. "I'm disappointed in you."

"Why?"

"This morning we brought in some cowboys to demonstrate the fine art of calf roping for our guests. You were noticeably absent."

Yuri shrugged. "I slept in."

"After that, our guests were invited to watch some of the best barrel racers in the country do their stuff. You didn't bother to attend."

He shrugged again. "I was reading in my cabin."

"At noon we had a friendly picnic lunch, with the cowboys and cowgirls as our special guests. One of the cowboys showed us some fancy rope tricks. You missed it."

"I wasn't hungry so I stayed in my cabin and caught up on some more of my reading."

"And now we're having some rousing games of horseshoe pitching and fast-draw target practice." She glanced at the pay phone. "And you're calling Houston to check up on your work."

"I don't like horseshoe pitching and I don't like guns."

"Is there *anything* you'd like to do?" Banner turned to him, exasperation clearly written on her face, then she shook her head when she saw the sensuous gleam enter his eyes. "Besides *that*," she added with a laugh. "Seriously, you're making us look bad. We've never had a guest so hard to please. At the risk of repeating myself, why did you come here?" She spread out her hands in a helpless gesture, and there was a plea in her voice. "The other guests asked if you were ill. So you see? Your absence hasn't gone unnoticed."

He leaned back against the house and shoved his hands into his trouser pockets. Despondency lined his face and dipped his mouth into a scowl. "I guess I don't know how to vacation. I didn't want to take two weeks off from work, but they made me."

"That's a first! Most people look forward to their vacation time."

"Not me. It's a waste, and I've wasted too much time already."

"Is this the same man who lectured me about exploring new places and breaking out of my routine?"

He laughed, realizing that she was right. "Tell you what," he said, turning toward her. "There *is* something I'd like to do."

"What?"

"I'd like you to show me your favorite place on the ranch. You've lived here all your life, so there must be some place off the beaten track that you save for yourself."

"A private tour, is that it?"

"Yes."

Banner considered his request for a few moments, finding it both tantalizing and perilous. She wanted to be alone with him. She had admitted that to herself last night when sleep had eluded her for hours while she relived every minute she'd spent with him.

There was a stamp of individuality about him that she appreciated. She smiled, noticing how everyone else was dressed in jeans, boots and Western shirts. Yuri had chosen khaki trousers, deck shoes and a mossy-green shirt. He didn't follow the crowd, and he didn't give a hang whether or not the crowd followed him. He was a man who set his own course his own way.

"Well?" Yuri goaded her.

"I've never given a private tour to anyone," she mused aloud.

"Won't you make an exception?" He leaned one hand on the wall behind her and delivered one of his most appealing smiles. "I'll pay extra for the experience."

She ducked under his arm, all too aware of the milling guests and curious glances. "That's okay. I'll give you a private tour without any extra charge for the services. Let's saddle up."

"Oh, no," he groaned, turning toward her with a heavy sigh. "Not horses again!"

"This is a dude ranch, Yuri," she reminded him.

"Yes, but I was hoping to avoid horses today." He hunched his shoulders and winced. "I'm giving my poor battered body a rest."

She eyed him speculatively and decided he deserved a break. "Okay, we'll take the pickup."

"Now you're talking," he said, draping a casual arm about her shoulders and moving with her toward the red pickup. He opened the driver's side and helped her up into the seat, then went around and got in on the passenger's side. "Where are we headed?"

"To my castle in the sky," she said, starting the pickup and steering it over the cattle guard.

"That sounds nice."

"It is. It's been my special place since I was six. I go there to sort out my problems and find peace of mind."

He angled himself against the door so that he could watch the sunlight flit over her face. She looked fresh as a daisy in a pair of white jeans and a yellow blouse that had puffed, off-the-shoulder sleeves. Her dark hair was gathered by a yellow bow at the nape of her neck. She wore no makeup except for a touch of lip gloss, letting her natural beauty shine through.

"Did you have a special place when you were a kid?" she asked, glancing at him.

"Yes. We lived in an apartment building and I liked the shadowy place under the stairs." A shudder coursed through him when he remembered another dark, dank place. "I don't like dark places anymore, though."

"Why not?"

He turned his head and gazed at the prairie as it slipped past the truck. "Dark places remind me of the ship's cargo hold."

"The ship..." Her voice faded, then came back. "Oh, when you were smuggled out of Russia?"

"Yes. I was in a crate and it was dark and cold."

"How long were you in the crate?"

"Too long." The memory of that time grew strong within him. "Let's talk about something else." He felt her worried glance, but ignored it.

"Why did you want to leave Russia? Is it really as bad as we're told it is?"

"No, it's a beautiful country filled with good people."

"Then why did you want to leave if it's so great?" she asked.

He regarded her carefully, noting the firm set of her lips and the death grip she had on the steering wheel. Russia was a sore spot with her. Any mention of it, especially in flattering tones, brought up her shields. Diana, Vladimir and Russia were the same ball of wax as far as Banner was concerned. It was time for her to put away her childish notions, he decided.

"Just what have you got against the Soviets, Banner?"

"I...I don't know what you mean."

"Every time I mention my native country you act as if I'm talking about purgatory. I admire patriotism, but you're taking it too far. You're taking it personally, aren't you?"

"Maybe," she hedged, glancing at him to find that he was regarding her with nerve-tingling intensity. She smiled, unwilling to dredge up gloomy things on a such a beautiful day. "Tell me about your work."

"My work?" He laughed, shaking his head a little. "Are you sure you want to hear about it?"

"Of course! What made you decide to be an engineer?"

"Flight has always fascinated me," he said, craning his neck to watch a bird sail above the pickup. "When I was a child I wanted to fly. I would watch the birds and flap my arms, but to no avail. The first time I saw an airplane I wanted to know everything about it."

"Did you make model airplanes?"

"Hundreds of them," he said, remembering those sweet, uncomplicated years of discovery. "What about you? What fascinated you as a child?"

She steered the truck off the road and through a pasture. "There wasn't one thing," she said, realizing that her childhood dreams had changed like the seasons. "I wanted to do everything. If I read a book about pirates I wanted to be a pirate, until I read another book about teachers and then I wanted to be a teacher. I never settled on one, but embraced them all."

"You had an active imagination?"

"Overactive," she amended. "I think I spent the first ten years of my life in a dreamland." She stopped the truck and pointed to a big elm. "And that's where I dreamed. There's a tree house up there that my dad built for me, and I've spent a good part of my life up there with the leaves and the clouds and my imagination."

"Will you take me up there?" Yuri asked, wanting to see this place of dreams.

"Sure." She smiled faintly before opening the truck door. "You'll be my first visitor. I never allowed anyone up there when I was a kid."

He was uncommonly pleased by her invitation. Nothing she could have done would have made him feel more privileged. He got out of the truck and followed her to the base of the tree. He could see a platform up through the leafy branches.

"It's big," he said, angling his head this way and that to see the dimensions of the tree house.

"It's a double-decker," she said proudly, then pointed to rungs tacked onto the trunk. "Use these to get up to that first branch and then make like a monkey. I'll go first to show you the way."

"Good." Yuri placed his hands at her waist to steady her as she made her way up the trunk.

When she swung up to the branch, then up to the next one, he shook his head in admiration. He followed with less certainty, preparing himself for the snap of a branch. Relief embraced him when he reached the tree-house landing. Banner pointed to the upper level, which was only half the size of the first.

"That level's gotten a little shaky over the years, but this one's still as sturdy as the day it was built." She sat down and motioned for him to sit beside her. "What do you think of my hideaway?"

"It's charming." Yuri sat next to her and looked around. A cardinal spotted him and flew away, crying out to its friends that this tree wasn't safe anymore. "I suppose you know every inch of your property."

"Oh, yes." She leaned back on stiff arms. "Every nook and cranny. There's a cave on the north-forty that I used to explore, but we boarded it up when we started the dude ranch. Dad said that most kids weren't as fearless as I was and they might wander into the cave and get scared."

Yuri nodded, imagining the dark, wet walls. His chest grew tight as claustrophobia wound through him with the finesse of a cobra. He directed his gaze to the sky, needing the security of wide open spaces.

"I like your dream house," he said, and was rewarded with a sincere smile.

"Yes, that's it," she agreed. "It's more than a tree house. It's a dream house."

"Your dreams must have been enough for you, since you've stayed here all your life."

"This ranch has always been my anchor," she said, tipping back her head to look up through the branches. "When I went to Oklahoma City I thought I'd be so homesick...."

"But you weren't?"

"Not really. I missed Dad, but I had so much fun!"

"What sort of schooling did you take?"

"Bookkeeping," she said with a wrinkle of her nose. "Secretarial school."

"Why that?"

She shrugged and lay flat on the planked floor. "Dad was never very good with figures, and I decided that I could help him more by going off to school and learning about finances and budgeting and all that stuff. It's come in handy. Things turned around for us when I finished school and came back home." She rolled her eyes expressively. "I took a look at his financial ledgers and wondered how in the world we'd kept things afloat! The first thing I did was to reduce the staff from fifteen to five, and then I raised the guest fees. Dad wasn't too crazy about that, but I knew we were underpriced. That first year after I took over the finances we cleared three thousand."

"I'm impressed," Yuri said, easing himself back until he was lying on his side next to her. He propped his head in his hand, feeling lazy and at ease with her. "Tell me about Oklahoma City. How long were you there?"

"Only three months, but it was wonderful! I lived in an apartment, near the school, with three other girls. We fixed each other up with dates and had so much fun. I felt so...so..."

"Free," Yuri said, and Banner nodded.

"Yes. I discovered that I have an aptitude for math. For a while I thought about continuing at the school and becoming an accountant." She glanced at him apprehensively. "I know that doesn't sound ambitious to you, but accounting interests me. I love to work with math. There isn't any guessing. It's either wrong or right."

"What do you think I do for a living?" he asked, chuckling. "I work with math day in, day out. If anyone can understand your interest in it, I can!"

She looked at him with a mixture of chagrin and embarrassment. "Of course. I didn't think..." Her voice trailed away, then came back strong and sure. "Most people think that accounting and bookkeeping are dull."

"Not me. Why don't you pursue it? You can go back to school and get your certification. Nothing's stopping you."

"I'm doing what I want to do," she said, but her tone lacked conviction. She shifted onto her side to face him. "Tell me more about your job, or is it top secret?"

"Some of it is," he said with a teasing grin. "Most of it, however, is public record. Besides working on long-range projects like the space stations, I also design satellites."

"Did you do the same sort of work in Russia?"

"No." He pursed his lips and diverted his gaze from hers. "I worked on weaponry back then. I didn't like it."

"Then why did you do it?"

He smiled at her innocence. "I wasn't given a choice. You have a saying here—necessity is the mother of invention. Well, I believe that imagination is the mother of invention."

Banner narrowed her eyes, giving him a stern look. "You're so driven! When you talk about your work you get so serious and... and almost desperate! I think you expect too much of yourself."

"And I think you expect too little of yourself," he countered, bringing an immediate frown to her soft mouth. "Uh-oh. She's mad again."

"I'm not mad," she insisted, sitting up and turning away from him. "But you're wrong about me."

"How can you look at that sky and not want to spread your wings and fly away?"

"Unlike you, I love my home and feel no need to escape it."

He winced, but conceded the point. "Let's not dwell on our differences when we have so much in common."

"Like what?" she asked. "Besides our being as stubborn as mules?"

He moved closer, placing one hand on her arm and forcing her around to him. "We're both single, over twenty-one and free to do whatever we wish with whomever we wish." He could resist her soft mouth no longer, but she drew back when his lips touched hers. "Remember when I asked you if you believed in destiny?"

"Yes," she murmured, keeping her gaze downcast.

"You said that you didn't, but I don't believe you. I was drawn here for reasons I couldn't explain until I saw you."

"Yuri, you've been lonely since you came to America and I think you're confusing—"

"I haven't been *that* lonely," he interrupted with a chuckle. "Not so lonely that I'd wander to Oklahoma in search of an available woman!" He cupped her chin in his hand and made her look directly into his eyes. "You feel it, too," he insisted. "You didn't want to like me and you made that quite obvious."

"Hold on a minute! You didn't give me a chance to like you. You were rude and arrogant!"

"I still am, but you like me anyway."

"I like most people," she said, then placed her hand on his thigh and pushed herself up to her feet. "I've got to get back to my other guests."

Yuri sprang to his feet, irritated and disappointed by her abrupt dismissal. "What is it, Banner? Why won't you let me near you?"

"I don't know." Banner edged away from him, perplexed by her own need to distance herself from him. "There's something about you..." She looked at him warily, feeling as if a tug-of-war were going on inside her, with attraction at one end and doubt at the other. "My instincts tell me that there's more to you than meets the eye."

"What does that mean?" he asked, diverting his gaze from hers and wondering if she were so perceptive that she could sense his deceit.

She laughed and waved a dismissing hand. "It's probably not you. It's me. I told you I was going through a phase." She shrugged and started to climb down the tree.

"Banner," Yuri said, grabbing her arm. "I could help you. You're at a crossroads and I can help you find the right direction to take."

She studied him for a moment, then shook her head. "I don't think so. Thanks for your concern, but I'll find my own way by myself."

Yuri released her, letting her scurry down the tree. He sighed impatiently, angry at her for being so damned stubborn.

"You're a hard woman to get close to, Banner O'Bryan!" he called down to her. "But I haven't given up."

"Come on down, Yuri," she shouted up to him. "Time to leave the land of dreams and get your feet back on solid ground."

He looked down at her sweet, beautiful face and felt ashamed for deceiving her. She'd hate him once he told her that he was Vladimir's son, but he'd hate himself if he didn't.

Four

"This is the best fishing hole on the property," Banner said, raising her voice so that she could be heard by all the guests who were seated along the banks of the pond. "So, no excuses if you don't catch anything, because this pond is stocked with catfish and perch."

"Y'all better get busy," Pete chimed in. "We're having fish for dinner. That means that if you don't catch 'em then it's bread and water tonight."

"For those of you that don't like fishing, there's a log cabin over that rise," Banner said, pointing to the south, where the land swelled. "It's been there for almost a hundred years and was built by the Stewart family. They were some of the first settlers in these parts and came by covered wagon from Virginia. Feel free to go inside the house and see how the folks lived back then. There's a collection of cooking and farming utensils inside that date back to the early eighteen hundreds."

Most of the guests started for the rise, their curiosity piqued. Only a few remained by the pond.

"Is fishing part of the dude ranch experience?" Yuri asked Banner as he sat beside her on the grassy bank.

"It sure is. Actually, it's our way of giving everybody a rest, since we'll be taking our longest trail ride tomorrow." She dropped a line into the water and leaned back on her elbows. "All the way to Fort Gibson. It's quite a ride, but worth it."

"Just what I need. Another long trail ride." Yuri selected a pole and baited the hook.

Banner nodded appreciatively. "You've been fishing before."

"Yes, my grandfather taught me."

Banner smiled. Things weren't that different on the other side of the world, she thought, then settled back and watched the fishing lines glint in the sun.

"Tell me about yourself," she said, wanting to know more about his life then and now.

"Let's talk about you."

Banner shook her head. "I've talked enough. It's your turn."

"We seem to be at a standoff." He shifted onto his side and looked at her. "I'll tell you about you and you tell me about me."

"What?" she asked, laughing at the idea. "That should be a short conversation. We know very little about each other."

"We might surprise each other. Want to try?"

"Sure. Why not?" She poked a finger into his shoulder. "You go first."

"All right."

Banner waited while the silence was stretched taut. She glanced at him and saw that his face was set in thoughtful lines. "Are you stumped already?"

"No, I'm gazing into my crystal ball." He closed his eyes for a moment, then gave a short, decisive nod. "Okay. You had an idyllic life when you were a child, since you were the only little girl for miles around." He swept one arm to encompass the green, rolling countryside. "You were such a beautiful child that it was easy to spoil you."

Banner smiled ruefully, but mentally agreed with his assessment.

"You probably learned to ride a horse at the same time you learned to walk. That's obvious by the way you handle yourself on a horse; it's second nature to you. How am I doing so far?"

"So far, so good," she allowed.

He tested his line before he continued, "Then your beautiful world collapsed and you were thrown into confusion. When the dust settled, you realized that your father had suffered a great loss and you wanted to ease his suffering."

"How dramatic!" Banner quipped, trying to lessen the uneasiness she was feeling. His serious expression made her more fidgety, and she focused her attention on the shimmering fishing line instead of the probing eyes.

"After your mother left, you and your father tried to pick up the pieces and get on with living. You secretly hoped that your father would meet another woman who would help him forget his broken marriage, but it was obvious that he wasn't interested in finding a replacement because he still loved your mother. He probably hoped that she would come back to him one day."

"A hopeless romantic," Banner said to herself, then realized she had spoken aloud. "I'm sorry. Go on. This is fascinating."

"Well, let's see... I would imagine that you spent most of your time trying to make restitution for your mother's desertion. You felt sorry for your father and you tried to make him happy. You were so intent on making him happy that you neglected your own life. In short, I think you're only now coming to realize that you've done yourself a disservice. By taking responsibility for something that wasn't your fault, you've put your life on hold."

Banner moved her baited hook to a different spot and concentrated on keeping her face expressionless. He was uncanny in his assessment of her life, and she felt exposed and vulnerable. "Finished?"

"Yes. How did I do?"

She selected her words carefully. "I'll withhold judgment for now."

"That's encouraging."

"It is?"

"Yes. A couple of days ago you wouldn't have withheld your judgment on anything I said. You would have given me directions to a cliff and pushed me over it."

"Oh, come on," Banner chided gently. "I wasn't that mean to you."

"You weren't that nice to me, either."

She shrugged off his comment. "It's my turn to talk about you. I hope you can take it as well as you can dish it out."

He squared his shoulders as if he were going into battle. "Ready. Give it your best shot."

She smiled, then concentrated on his noble profile and tried to glean something from it. "You're a puzzle, but I think I can fit a few pieces together. You had a happy childhood, too, but tragedy struck when your father left. I think he must have left without a trace, throwing your whole family into turmoil. You became the head of the family and tried in every way possible to help your mother cope with the situation." She paused, studying him minutely but failing to see any sign that she was on the right track.

She shook her head and stared blindly at the murky water.

"Well? Is that it?" Yuri asked.

"Give me a minute," Banner grumbled. "This isn't easy." She heaved a sigh and decided to go with her instincts. "Okay, here goes. You were never completely happy after your father left. You were restless and dissatisfied with the way your life was going. When your career stalled, you became frustrated and desperate. You began thinking of leaving the country." She paused, trying to put herself in his shoes. "I don't know the exact circumstances, but something happened—something cataclysmic—that forced you to make some difficult decisions. You decided to leave Russia, no matter the cost or danger to your own life." She angled a glance at him. "Am I warm?"

"I'm withholding judgment."

Banner slapped his bent knee playfully. "Copycat! This is silly. I'm probably way off base. One thing I'm certain about is that you're a workaholic."

"A what?" he asked, chuckling. "What am I?"

"A workaholic. You're addicted to your work," she explained. "You've forgotten how to have fun, how to relax, how to simply enjoy goofing off. Maybe you never learned how to let yourself go. I mean, you resent having to take a vacation! That's ridiculous!"

"Is there a cure for my condition?"

"You have to cure yourself. I don't mean to criticize...." She placed one hand on his forearm. "Being dedicated to your work is admirable, but not to the exclusion of everything else."

When his gaze lowered from her face to where her hand was clutching his forearm, Banner snatched her hand away, surprised by her own desperation to make him see the error of his ways. She laughed, trying to lighten the situation she'd made serious.

"I'm sorry. I sort of got carried away," she apologized.

"That's quite all right," he said in a voice that made her tingle. "I like being touched by you. I just wish you'd do it more often. Who knows? With enough tender loving care I might let myself go."

"You're such a tease," she said, still trying to laugh off the incident.

"No, you're the tease. You know that I want you, but you—"

"Yuri, don't." She put her fishing pole aside and stood up. "Not here. Not now."

"Very well." He got to his feet and looked toward the rise. "Let's go look at that cabin." He didn't wait for her to agree, but grasped one of her hands and pulled her along with him.

"Are you going to tell me if I was right about you?" she asked as they climbed the rise.

"No." He helped her down the other side, cupping his other hand under her elbow.

"Okay, I'll admit that you're right about most things." She smiled, tipping her head to one side and waiting for him to return the favor.

Yuri glanced up at the sky and sighed. "All right, you were right about me for the most part, but I have a good reason for working so hard."

"What reason?"

He curved an arm around her shoulders and guided her toward the cabin. "I sacrificed a lot by coming here, Banner. I feel as if I'm starting from scratch. Everyone else had a head start. I must run like the wind to catch up and make it all worthwhile."

"There's more to the good life than being successful in your career."

"Well, we all have our crosses to bear, don't we?"

She stopped, and his arm fell from her shoulders. "In other words, you think I'm not one to lecture you? This might come as a surprise to you, but I'm happy with my life."

"You're right. It does come as a surprise."

Banner pressed her lips together and spun away from him to glare at the rustic cabin. "This cabin was built when Oklahoma was Indian territory. The Stewart family—"

"I don't give a damn about that Stewart family," he said, catching one of her arms and whirling her around. His mouth flamed across hers, stealing away her breath and her protests.

Banner gripped his shoulders in surprise. Her fingers moved against his shirt, tracing muscle and bone, and a traitorous weakness stole through her. She didn't want to fight him anymore. She wanted to surrender and walk on the wild side of nature with him. He knew the way. He'd guide her.

He lifted his mouth from hers and smiled into her lustrous eyes. "Would you like to know what happened to make me decide to leave Russia?" He laughed when she nodded enthusiastically. "I thought that might get your attention." He nuzzled one corner of her mouth, and the tip of his tongue traced the crease. "Have you decided to quit fighting me? Have I finally worn you out?"

"Only for the moment," she said, sliding her hands down the front of his shirt and stepping back from him. "Were you in some kind of trouble in Russia?"

"No." He started strolling toward the cabin, and Banner walked with him. "It wasn't as dramatic as that. I was a good solid citizen. There were things about my home that I didn't particularly care for, but I was sophisticated enough to know that nowhere in the world is there a Utopia."

They'd reached the cabin and Yuri stepped inside. Banner followed, and the smell of fresh, damp earth was heavy in the air. Her feet sank into the sod floor that was strewn with hay.

"This is bleak," Yuri said, placing a hand on the rough walls. "An entire family lived in here?"

"Yes." Banner went to the single window. "See this roll of material?" she asked, lifting a hand to the stained cloth above the window. "They let this down at night to keep out insects and curious animals like raccoons." She untied the cloth. "It's so dark when this is down and the door is closed that you can't see your hand in front of your face."

"Please, leave it up," Yuri said, reaching her side and holding the cloth in place. "I prefer the sunlight." He tied the cloth in place, then took one of Banner's hands and led her outside again. "It smells better out here."

"You'd make a lousy pioneer," she admonished gently. "So you were a solid citizen in Russia. What happened to make you want to leave?"

He ran a hand over her head in a pretense of brushing a wayward strand of her black hair away from her face. "To be truthful, I'd thought about America since I was an adolescent. My father taught all of us English, except for my mother. She never wanted to learn. As I grew older I became more curious about the United States and its space program. I worked in the Soviet space program, but on a limited basis."

"Why limited?" Banner asked.

"Oh, for several reasons."

"That you're not going to reveal," Banner tacked on.

"It's hard to explain." He lifted a lock of her hair and let it slip through his fingers. "Your hair feels like silk."

"You were talking about leaving Russia," she reminded him, then reached up and combed his silky hair back from his forehead. "Yours feels like silk, too." When he leaned forward, she swayed back and laughed. "Tell me about why you left Russia."

He rocked his head to one side, looking at her in a contemplative way as if he were thinking about her as he answered. "I heard rumors of a transfer. No one would confirm it, but a couple of men I trusted told me that I was soon to be transferred out of the space program. I was to be sent to a small town near Leningrad to teach science to children."

"Just like that? Why would they waste your skills like that?"

"I suppose they had their reasons, but I knew that I couldn't go along with them. I wasn't that happy with my life as it was, and I knew I would be miserable teaching school and being away from my family." He fingered the collar of her shirt, then tucked his hand beneath it and curved his fingers along the side of her neck. "I decided that I had to act quickly. If I were to be sent away from my family and my home, then I would take matters into my own hands and control my own destiny."

There's that word again, Banner thought, but remained silent. Destiny seemed to play a large role in the life of Yuri Mytova.

"I had acquaintances in the American Embassy and I used them. I had money put aside and I used it. I bought my way out of Russia in a sense."

"Sounds easy, but I bet it wasn't."

"It wasn't that difficult," he said, frowning slightly as his gaze moved slowly, thoughtfully over her face. "It was just nerve-racking and frightening."

"Did you tell your family that you were leaving?"

"No." His frown deepened to a scowl and his gaze came to rest on her mouth. "The less they knew the better it would be for them. I hinted to my mother that I was unhappy and that I was being forced into a difficult decision. I think she knew what I was talking about. I think she had an understanding of what I was going through."

"She sounds like a wonderful woman," Banner murmured, but she was merely mouthing words. Her entire being was trembling with expectation. She wanted Yuri's mouth on hers, and she was only vaguely aware of slipping her hands around his neck and pulling his head down until his lips touched hers, lightly and lingeringly.

His hands spread across her throat, and his thumbs pressed against the pulses beneath her ears.

"Your heart beats as quickly as mine," he murmured against her mouth.

"Like a scared rabbit's," she whispered, loving the brush of her lips on his.

"Didn't you know that on the other side of fear is love?"

She gazed deeply into his eyes. Why was he talking about love? He didn't know her well enough to love her. But then she remembered his earlier assessment of her life and she realized that, in some ways, he knew her better than she knew herself.

"You baffle me," she admitted. "I don't know how to respond to you, or even if I should."

"Don't worry. I know exactly how to respond to you."

His lips warmed hers, then parted to suckle gently. He moistened her lips with his tongue until they glistened. Banner closed her eyes and tipped her head back, urging him to continue his tender seduction. His hands slid from her neck to her shoulders, and then his arms tightened around her. Banner parted her lips and Yuri's tongue entered her mouth, boldly and passionately. He kissed like no other man she'd known, sending her senses into an eddy. She was aware of her breasts flattening against his chest and the thrust of his hips against hers. Her hands drifted down his face and she felt the scrape of his whiskers against her palms and the flexing of his cheeks as his tongue moved back and forth on top of hers.

His hands hurried down her back and then spread over her hips, driving her closer to him until she felt his arousal and became aware of her own. When his lips moved to the side of her neck, finding tender patches of skin, Banner quaked with longing. She wanted him to make love to her more than anything she'd ever wanted in her life.

"Yuri, make—" The sound of her voice and the import of her request sent her from his arms. She stood a few steps from him, her eyes wide, her breathing ragged.

"Banner?" he asked, bewildered. "What's wrong?"

"You do frighten me," she said, laughing at her own reaction.

"Why?"

"Why?" she echoed, holding out her hands so that he could see how they were shaking. "I'm standing here trembling, and you ask me why?" She pushed her hair back from her face, then pressed her palms against her flushed cheeks. "Kissing you is like making love," she said, trying to make him understand how swept away she was... how close she was to total surrender. "And I'm not sure we should do that... make love, I mean." Her gaze rested on his mouth, which was moist from her kisses. She'd never seen a more irresistible mouth. "You have an unfair advantage," she murmured.

"Unfair..." He looked away from her. "I never meant to be unfair to you."

She shook her head, realizing that he was taking her comment too seriously. "It's only an expression. I didn't mean—"

"I don't want to hurt you," he said, his gaze fastening on hers again. "I don't want that, Banner."

"I know." She lifted her hands and let them fall in a hapless gesture. "I guess I'm making a big deal out of this, but it is a big deal. I've never felt this way about a man. I'm not exactly a woman of the world." She wrinkled her nose playfully. "I guess you noticed that, right?"

He stepped closer and his fingertips trailed from the corner of her eye to the beauty mark on her left cheekbone.

"It's one of the things I find most endearing about you." He kissed the beauty mark, then straightened with resolve. "Let's join the others."

"Yes." Banner laughed nervously and linked her arm in his. "I think that would be best, under the circumstances." She held back a moment, making him look at her. "Yuri, I'm glad you came here. We got off to a shaky start and I'm still confused as to why you decided to visit the ranch, but I'm thankful you did."

She smiled, expecting him to reward her with a kiss or some tender words of gratitude, but instead he looked as if she'd slapped him hard across the face.

"Yuri?" She stepped in front of him, placing her hands on his forearms and holding him in place. "What's wrong? I only meant—"

"I know what you meant," he interrupted. He smiled, but it never reached his eyes. He gripped her shoulders and turned her around, then gave her a little push. "You're neglecting your other guests, Miss O'Bryan. Better get a move on."

"I feel as if I've been dismissed," she said, throwing a frown at him over her shoulder.

"Only postponed," he assured her, and she seemed satisfied with that.

Banner entered the gleaming kitchen to the rattle of pots and pans. Cookie paused in loading the commercial-size dishwasher to glance at Banner before he turned back to his work.

"Evening, Banner," he said. "That fish dinner tasted good, didn't it?"

"Nobody can fry up fish like you, Cookie," she said, pleased to see him grin at her compliment. "What's on tomorrow's menu?"

"Big trail ride tomorrow, right?" Cookie asked, closing the dishwasher and punching buttons with his stubby fingers.

"Yes, so they'll need a rib-sticking breakfast and a packed lunch."

"I'll fry up some chickens," Cookie said, wiping his hands on his white apron. "Potato salad would go down good, and fresh fruit is easy to pack."

"Sounds great." Banner leaned close to the bearded man and lowered her voice to a conspiratorial whisper. "I swear, I think a lot of our return guests come back for your delicious meals."

Cookie chuckled, his blue eyes merry and twinkling. "Go on, now."

"No, really!" Banner nodded emphatically and gave him a hug. "How many of them asked for your hush puppies recipe tonight?"

"Quite a few," he said with a touch of pride. "But I never give away my secrets."

"Good idea." She kissed his whiskered cheek affectionately. "Someday you'll have to give me some lessons. I don't think I could boil water."

"You never had to try. Always had me around to fix your food."

"See you tomorrow, Cookie."

"You turning in already?"

"No. I'm going to change clothes and go over to the Shortbranch. I imagine most of the guests are there already."

"Have a good time." Cookie waved her off and lumbered over to the butcher block where hills of fruits and vegetables awaited him.

"Need any help?" Banner asked.

"No, you go on. Show those city slickers how to do the Texas two-step."

Banner pushed through the swinging doors and stepped blindly into Yuri. His arms came around her, steadied her, then remained at her waist.

"Nice running into you," he murmured.

"Same here." She glanced around at the empty corridor. "What are you doing here?"

"Looking for you. You always do a disappearing act after dinner, and I was wondering where you vanished to."

"My quarters usually. That's where I'm headed now, and then I thought I'd go over to the Shortbranch." When he didn't release her, she asked hesitantly, "Would you like to see my wing of the house?"

"I thought you'd never ask." He dropped his arms from her waist and extended a hand. "After you."

She led the way down the corridor, turned the corner and walked to the double doors leading into her office. "You know, I don't usually invite my guests into my inner sanctum."

"I'm honored." He reached past her and opened one of the doors. "Where do the others live?"

"Cookie has a couple of rooms off the kitchen. Pete and the other hands live in a bunk house." She laughed when Yuri made a dire face. "It's not as bad as it sounds. It's a big building and each hand has his own room. Of course, Pete will move in with DiDi once they're married. DiDi lives in the cottage behind this house."

"When's the wedding?"

"The latest I've heard is the Fourth of July."

"Independence Day," Yuri observed. "That's a strange day for a wedding."

"Not really," Banner disagreed as she unlocked the door to her quarters. "Marriage doesn't necessarily mean you're giving up your independence."

"What does it mean then?"

Banner opened the door and switched on the lamp. "Fidelity." Her gaze swung automatically to the painting above the fireplace. "It means that you've chosen someone to spend the rest of your life with."

"Forsaking all others?" Yuri asked behind her.

"Exactly."

Yuri walked past her, stopping in the center of the living room to admire the watercolor rendition of the Rocking Horse compound.

"Your mother painted this."

Banner nodded, noting that he hadn't asked but had stated it for fact. "I believe it's the only landscape she ever painted. She was known for her still lifes and portraits."

"You kept it." His voice reflected amazement. "In spite of your feelings for her, you kept it."

"I had no choice."

"There's always a choice."

Banner conceded his point. "Yes. I wanted to donate it to a museum but Dad threw a fit when I suggested it. He made me promise that I'd never get rid of it. After he died, I thought about storing it in the attic, but it reminds me as much of him as it does her." She shrugged helplessly. "Dad said it was the only thing he had left of her."

"It sounds to me as if she was your father's obsession."

"There was something about her..." Banner's voice trailed off as vague memories surfaced. "She was a beautiful woman. What I remember most about her was her voice. It was melodic and her laughter sounded like music. She used to read stories to me and she made them come alive with her voice." Banner stepped closer to the painting, drawn by the memories. "There are women who are hard to forget. I guess she was one of them."

"How did she meet your father?"

Banner smiled sadly. "She told me about that. Dad never talked much about her to me. They met through an advertising agency." Banner laughed, imagining that first meeting. Such an odd couple. "Dad had been selected from hundreds of cowboys to be on a poster advertising a brand of cigarettes, and Mother had been commissioned to paint him. By the time the painting was finished Dad was hopelessly in love with her."

"And she with him," Yuri added.

"Well, I'm not so sure about that." Banner crossed her arms, hugging herself and warding off the impending memories. "I think she had some romantic notions about living on a ranch. She was flighty, winging from one romantic fantasy to another." Sadness coated her and she turned away from the painting. "Promises meant nothing to her. She'd vowed to love my father and stay with him for better or worse."

"You're an intolerant woman, Banner." He ignored her pointed glare and continued to scrutinize the painting. "What is it that the American Indians said? Something about not passing judgment on a man until you've walked a mile in his shoes? Wise advice."

"You think I've judged her too harshly?"

He pulled his gaze from the painting and faced her. "I think you've dwelt too much on your past...on your parents' past." He spread out his hands. "Things happen. People change. Promises are broken. That's life, Banner."

"Dad missed her terribly—tragically." She blinked, realizing that her voice was dropping along with her mood. Squaring her shoulders, she pushed aside her gloomy thoughts and pirouetted. "Well, this is my modest home. Is it more or less what you expected?"

He didn't answer immediately, but strolled around the room, stopping occasionally to examine certain items: her father's spurs mounted on the wall, a worn, rawhide easy chair, a photo of Lucas O'Bryan and Cookie.

"I don't see much of you in this room," he observed. "This is a man's room."

His observation startled her, and she looked around the room with a fresh insight. He was right. This room had been decorated by Lucas O'Bryan. Banner's touch was nowhere in sight.

"Where's your bedroom?"

"My bedroom?" Banner repeated. She hadn't meant to give him such a thorough tour. She'd thought he'd be satisfied to see the living room. Unerringly, her gaze slid toward the door on the right of the fireplace.

"Here?" he asked, moving in that direction and reaching for the doorknob.

"Yes, but it's just your regular garden variety..." She didn't bother to finish the sentence, since Yuri had already opened the door and encroached on her private world.

His eyes widened and he smiled before striding across the threshold. Banner followed, wanting to see what had brought that beatific grin to his face. He pressed his fingertips against the blue satin comforter on her four-poster bed and sighed as if he had found a pot of gold.

"Now this room is yours. You're scattered all over it. Here," he said, running one hand across the comforter, then touching a lacy lamp shade. "And here." He went to the dresser where perfume bottles and jewelry boxes shared space with a makeup mirror, brushes and combs. "You're here, and over there in that vase of wildflowers." He swept a hand in the direction of the living room. "That room smells of leather and pipes. This room smells of flowers and sachets."

Banner enjoyed the expression on his face as he went back to the bed and sat on it. He ran his hands over the quilted satin, and took a deep breath that stretched the material of his black pullover.

"I can smell you," he said, his enigmatic gaze finding hers. "And this," he said, stroking the comforter again, "this is the same color as your eyes."

She went to him, reaching out a hand to pluck at the sleeve of his black sweater. "And this is the color of your eyes right now. They're dark brown, but most of the time they look black." She pushed her fingers through his hair. "Black like your hair. My dark Russian." She smiled, liking the sound of that and its implications. She bent over and kissed his parted lips. "Do you know that you're the first man to sit on my bed?"

"I don't believe it," he said, shaking his head. "I'm sure you've had at least one gentleman caller before me."

"Yes, but not in here. This has always been my private place. Of course, I didn't invite you in here. You just barged right in."

"If I had waited for an invitation I'd still be standing in your living room. Sometimes a man has to take matters in his own hands."

"Oh, yes," Banner murmured as her eyes closed and her lips opened to the touch of his. His hands framed her face, pulling her forward. "Yes, yes," she chanted, angling her body sideways to sit in his lap. Her arms slipped around his neck, his around her waist, and his mouth opened to take her in.

Desire thundered through her and she gave herself up to it. His tongue entered her mouth, moving sensuously in a way that made Banner wiggle in his lap. His hands moved up her back, then back down to her hips. With a moan, he lay back on the bed and took Banner with him. She slid her body on top of his and explored the contours of his face with her fingertips. Her lips moved to the side of his neck where the scent of his after-shave was strong. She ran her tongue along a vein in his neck, smiling against his skin when he shivered.

Years of holding herself on a tight rein made her new sense of freedom all the more precious. When his hands slipped under her sweater to caress her warm skin, Banner caught them and moved them around to her breasts. She sat astride him, lifting her upper body so that his hands could cover her breasts. Her nipples grew hard against his palms, and Banner gripped his wrists and moved his hands up and down against her.

Yuri pushed up her sweater to expose her breasts to his seeking gaze. He rose up and his mouth enveloped one. His tongue circled her nipple, then scraped across it. Banner moaned, her hands sliding up his hair-roughened forearms as her lower body began to tremble.

She kissed his neck, felt the rapid flutter of his pulse, and was thrilled to discover that he was as swept away as she.

"Yuri," she murmured, almost mindless with desire, "this is so right, isn't it?"

She didn't need his assurance, but she wanted it. She wanted him to tell her that she was special, wonderful, unforgettable. He was those things to her. She'd known it that day in the stables when he'd stormed her defenses and made her wary of him... of the passion he could stir within her. It's fate, she thought. Just like he said. We're meant to be. Destined for love.

"Banner, please..." His voice drifted to her, and she responded to his plea by molding her mouth to his and seeking the answering stroke of his tongue.

He tore his lips from hers. "Banner, please. Listen to me...."

"Yuri, it's okay," she whispered, pressing kisses to his forehead and high cheekbones. "Don't you know that I'm falling in love with you?"

"Banner, please!" His hands, which had been so gentle and encouraging, closed like vises on her forearms and held her away from him. "I...I can't do this!" He shoved her sideways and sprang from the bed.

"You can't do what?" Banner asked, tugging her sweater back in place.

He shook his head and combed his fingers through his mussed hair. "This isn't right."

"Not right?" She stood before him, so angry that she wanted to pummel him with her fists. "Let me get this straight. You've led me on and on and now you're telling me that you don't want me after all?"

"No, that's not what I'm saying." His voice was shaky, uncertain.

"Who do you think you are? You can't toy with my feelings like this!" She pushed him back and went to the door. "Get out!"

"There's something I should tell you before this goes any further."

"This isn't going any further. Go!" She pointed him in the right direction.

"Banner, you don't understand."

"I understand that you're having second thoughts."

He held out his hands, appealing to her. "I thought that it wouldn't matter to me...but it does."

"What's wrong, Yuri? Did I goof up and take your advances too seriously? Do you have a guilty conscience? Tough!"

"I do have a guilty conscience, but—"

"Why don't you just leave?"

He hesitated for a few moments, then heaved a sigh and strode from the bedroom.

"I can't talk sense to you when you're like this," he shouted over his shoulder at her. "But I *will* talk to you, Banner, and you *will* listen!"

"Don't bet on it!"

He slammed the living room door behind him, and Banner shut the bedroom door with enough force that the bottles of perfume on her dresser danced, and one almost tipped over.

Five

The bartender at the Shortbranch Saloon set the stein of beer in front of Yuri, then pushed a bowl of peanuts closer to him.

"You being from Russia, I'd a thought you'd order a vodka," the bartender said, chuckling at his joke.

Yuri forced a smile. "I've become Americanized." He hoisted the stein in a silent salute then took a long swallow. Yuri wiped flecks of foam from his upper lip as the bartender moved away.

The saloon was noisy with blaring music from a jukebox and whoops and hollers from the customers, but Yuri tuned out the din and gathered his depression around him like a tarnished shield. He glanced at his wristwatch, counting down the minutes as he finished the beer. He'd give her a half hour to settle herself, and then he'd call and warn her that he was coming over. That was the plan. Simple. Complicated. Sane. Insane.

"How about another one, partner?" the bartender asked, eyeing Yuri's half-empty stein.

"No, thanks. Have to keep my wits about me."

"Aw, come on. You're on vacation. Live it up!"

"Some vacation." Yuri frowned and drank the last of the beer.

"Aren't you having fun?" the bartender asked, leaning an arm on the bar and giving Yuri a look of concern. "We don't like to see frowns around this place, partner. It's not good for business."

Yuri checked his watch again. It seemed as if he'd spent a day in this place instead of only fifteen minutes.

"Got an appointment?" the bartender asked.

"Yes." Yuri slid off the stool. "Here you go." He tossed a bill onto the shiny bar. "Keep the change."

"Thanks, partner."

Yuri grimaced. He wasn't in the mood for folksy concern. Minutes ago he'd shattered what could have been a wonderful relationship—perhaps the relationship of a lifetime. He didn't feel like anybody's partner.

He went toward the bat-wing doors, stopping at the white telephone near them. After reading the instructions on the wall above it, he lifted the receiver and waited.

"Ranch operator," a perky voice announced.

"DiDi? This is Yuri."

"Hiya! What can I do you for?" she asked, giggling. "Just kidding, Yuri. What do you need?"

Yuri grimaced again. Was everyone giddy tonight? "Put me through to Banner's quarters, please."

"You mean her private wing?"

"Yes." He waited, sensing DiDi's hesitation. "DiDi, please put me through. It's okay. I'm sure she's expecting my call."

"Oh. Okay."

The phone rang twice before it was answered.

"Yes?"

Yuri gripped the receiver and took a deep breath. "Banner, it's me. Don't hang up!" He waited a second to make sure she hadn't, then rushed on with a speech he'd rehearsed since he'd left her quarters minutes ago. "I'm coming over to talk to you...to explain. Banner, you'd better let me in or I'll kick open the door." He hung up, closed his eyes with relief, and wondered if his voice had been gruff enough to convince her to let him in. Well, he'd soon find out, he thought, as he pushed through the saloon's traditional bat-wing doors and strode into the night.

With each step his mind chanted, "Stupid, stupid, stupid" into his ear. As he neared the main house, perspiration coated his skin and his heart hammered against his rib cage. How to tell her? Gently? Roundabout? Bluntly? It didn't matter how he told her, only that he told her.

He shouldn't have let it get this far, he scolded himself. He shouldn't have gone into her bedroom and coaxed her into his lap. That had been his undoing. Holding her, kissing her, caressing her... it had been more than his conscience could take. And when she'd said that she was falling in love with him—well, that had been like a sheet of cold water thrown on him. She was falling in love with him. He was falling in love with her. How did it ever get this complicated?

"Stupid," he bit out, then bounded up on the porch and into the lobby. The door banged behind him, sounding like a shotgun's report.

DiDi was at the operator's panel and she nearly jumped out of her skin. She laughed, holding a hand against her heart. "Lordy, you scared me! Hello again. Are you okay?" Her green eyes narrowed. "You look...so pale!"

"I'm fine." He walked past her, through the lobby and toward Banner's office.

"Uh...Yuri!" DiDi's voice rang with alarm. "Is she—?"

"She's expecting me," he said without turning around, then he opened the door and strode through the office. He lifted a fist and pounded on the door to her quarters. "Banner! I mean it! Let me—"

The door swung open and Banner arched one brow in haughty ridicule. "Come in, and please lower your voice a few decibels. There's no need to broadcast your explanation, is there?"

He stepped back, momentarily thrown out of kilter by her outward calm, but then he saw the smokiness in her sapphire eyes and he knew it was just that—an *outward* calm. The lady was steamed.

She'd changed from her jeans and sweater into a white dressing gown, and Yuri wished she hadn't done that. She looked too cool, too tantalizing, too pure. In contrast, he felt too hot, too tantalized, too tainted.

"Well," she said in an icy voice, "are you coming in or not?"

"I'm in," he said, stepping over the threshold. His gaze followed her as she moved past him to the mantel. She turned around to face him, leaning her shoulders against the polished wood. He had to hand it to her. She had gotten herself together a lot faster than he had.

"Tell me your story, then get out." She lifted a hand to hide her yawn. "I'm tired and I have to be up by six tomorrow."

"I hate to bore you any further," he shot back with sharp sarcasm. She was getting to him, making him angry, putting him at a further disadvantage.

"Then I'll save you the trouble. I've figured you out all by myself. You lied to me." She smiled coldly when he expressed surprise. "You see? I might be just a country girl, but I'm not stupid." She held out one hand to examine her fingernails, but mostly to avoid his eyes. "You're married, right? You thought you could have a vacation fling, but your conscience got in the way. Is she in Houston or Moscow?"

He slumped his shoulders and ran a hand down his face. Mirthless laughter scraped his throat like sandpaper and she glared grimly at him.

"I'm not married, but I did lie to you."

She dropped her hand and all pretense. "If you're not married, then what? What have you been keeping from me?"

"May I sit down?"

"No. You can tell me the truth and then leave." She folded her arms across her breasts and tapped one blue slipper on the oval rug.

"It hasn't all been lies," he said, avoiding the moment when she would gaze at him with hatred instead of contempt. "We have a lot in common, you and I. We're both from broken homes...." He looked at the painting above her and wished that he'd never read about Diana. "Do you know very much about the man your mother had an affair with?"

"Not much. I know that he was a home wrecker."

He winced and closed his eyes to ward off the desire to shake her.

"Will you get to the point?"

"Yes. I know I'm avoiding the truth." He shrugged helplessly, wishing he could kiss her once more before he ruined everything. "It's just that you're so beautiful and I—"

"Spare me your hollow compliments, Yuri." She turned sideways and stared at the empty, charred grate. "I admit that your pretty words turned my head once, but no more. Just say what you came to say and cut the fat off it."

"The man who fell in love with your mother—"

"My father, you mean?"

"No." He shook his head, more from irritation than denial. She was being obtuse and he knew it. "I meant—"

"That low-down, self-centered louse?" she cut in with an angry jeer. "He was Russian, like you."

Yuri tucked his fingers into his pockets so that she wouldn't see that they were trembling. He breathed deeply, feeling sick and weak, then he forced himself to look at her. Her blue eyes mocked him, driving a knife through his heart.

"Like father, like son," he said, only managing a whisper. "Yes?"

Time seemed to slow to half-speed, etching every nuance of her expression in Yuri's mind. Her eyes reflected nothing at first, then confusion, then disbelief. Her hands lifted and her fingertips touched her lips as they parted, pressed together, and parted again. She reached out blindly to grasp the mantel to keep herself upright when her knees seemed to give way.

"W-what did you say?" Her voice wasn't strong anymore. It was no more than a breath of sound.

Yuri prepared himself for the raging storm of emotions, bracing his feet apart and squaring his shoulders.

"He was my father, Banner. My name isn't Mytova. It's Yuri Zaarbo."

Her eyes closed slowly and she seemed to wilt before his eyes. She rounded her shoulders as her head sagged forward. Only her clutching fingers on the mantel kept her from falling to her knees.

"Your... father," she whispered in a dull, aching voice.

"Yes. I should have told you from the start, but I didn't think... well, I didn't know how I'd feel about you. I thought I'd come here, meet you and go away without getting involved in any real sense."

"Hit and run. I get it."

"No, you don't." He took a step toward her, but stopped when her eyes flew open and her head snapped up. Her actions told him to keep his distance, and he heeded them. "I didn't want to hurt you, Banner. We have so much in common and I wanted to—"

"We have nothing in common!" Her voice was shrill and her eyes blazed with the hatred he had feared. "You have nerve! What possessed you to come here? I've spent years trying to exorcise the name Zaarbo from my life! Why did you come back to haunt me? I thought I was rid of you!"

He didn't like the way she'd fused him and his father together, making them one and the same.

"I'm not him. I'm just his son."

"You're just like him!" She balled her hands into fists and leaned forward with a fervent intensity. "You think you have a right to wreak havoc in people's lives! Well, you don't! I won't let you hurt me anymore. Do...you...hear...me?" she asked, taking one step for each word until her face was inches from his. Her lips inched back to reveal her clenched teeth. "I won't let you! Now are you going to leave or do I have to get Pete in here to throw out the garbage?"

He was surprised that he could smile, but he did, although it felt false on his lips. "I'll leave," he said simply, then turned and went to the door. He paused and looked back at her. She was staring bullets at him. "There's more that you should know, but I can tell that you don't want to listen. You'd rather remain in your misinformed, misdirected world." He dipped his head in a solemn salute. "Fine. Goodbye."

Then he left her with his dreams scattered at her feet. It hadn't been destiny, after all, he thought. It had been foolishness.

The sky had begun to lighten, but it was still overcast and rainy, and Banner remained at the window seat and stared at the wet panes, following one drop after another on its journey to the sill.

She hadn't moved from the window since Pete had called at midnight to ask if they should postpone tomorrow's trail ride.

"Weatherman says it's going to rain cats and dogs, but it'll be nice and clear day after tomorrow," he'd reported.

"Yes, let's reschedule," Banner had agreed, grateful for the reprieve. She wouldn't be strong enough for the ride tomorrow anyway. "We'll let our farrier show them how to make horseshoes instead."

"Good idea. I'll call Blackie right now and tell him that he's on tomorrow. Night, hon."

Banner sighed away the snatch of memory and listened to the patter of rain. It wasn't a heavy downpour, but a constant mist. Her eyes were dry and her eyelids felt like weights. She blinked and could feel her lids scrape against her irises. She was bone tired, but unable to get her body to rest while her mind was still racing in circles.

Why? Why? Why?

It was her litany, a circle within a circle, going round and round with no stopping.

Why had he come? How much did he know? What had he wanted to tell her? Had he met her mother? Had he been close to his father? Had Vladimir told him about Diana? Why had he lied to her? What had he gained from it? Why did he confess? Did he have any feelings for her? Had she only imagined she'd seen tenderness and compassion in his eyes?

"Oh, the questions," she moaned, holding her aching head between her hands. "Stop, please stop."

But there was only one way to break free of the circle of questions. Only one way.

She looked at the clock and wasn't surprised to find that it was only a few hours from dawn. If she couldn't sleep, then perhaps he couldn't, either. If she waited until morning he might not be around. His goodbye had been final. He might have already packed and left the ranch.

Panic seized her and she sprang from the window seat and moved toward the door. She paused, looking down apprehensively at her dressing gown and slippers, then went to the closet and slipped on her raincoat and exchanged her slippers for rubbers. It was a weird outfit, but no one would be awake at this hour to see her. No one but him, if he were still in his cabin. Even if he wasn't, she'd wake him because she had to break through the circle to find peace of mind again.

She tiptoed through the house and outside into the chilly night. Spring was new and the nights still belonged to late winter. The ground glistened with moisture that was almost crystallized. She walked through patches of it that crunched under her feet and others that thoroughly drenched her galoshes. Her breath fogged in front of her nose and froze her lungs as she hurried through the mist toward Yuri's cabin. The other cabins she passed were dark, but there was a light in his bedroom window.

She'd been right. He was awake, too, trapped in the circle with her.

Banner went up the steps to the porch and tapped lightly on his door. She waited several seconds before she tapped again with more force. In the quiet night it sounded like a cannon blast, and she looked around furtively, expecting the lights in the other cabins to come on. When he still didn't answer, she applied the flat of her hand to the door several times and the door trembled on its hinges.

"What? Wait a second."

His drowsy voice drifted through the door. Banner heard his footsteps, then the lock shot back and the door opened.

She couldn't see his face, but she could tell that his hair was mussed and that he was pulling a robe around him.

"Banner... what the... what time is it?" His voice was hoarse, his words slurred and more accented than usual.

She pushed past him, then reached back and closed the door. "I saw your light and I thought you were still awake."

"My light..." He looked toward the bedroom where a path of pale yellow poured over the threshold. "Oh, right. No, I was asleep." He ran a hand down his face and heaved a sigh. "What's wrong? What time did you say it was?"

"Three."

"In the morning?" His voice broke and he cleared his throat. "Haven't you slept since...?"

"No," she answered his abbreviated question. "I haven't slept since you left. I'm surprised that you have, but then you're not the one who received the shock." She switched on a table lamp so that she could see him better. The skin around his eyes was puffy from sleep, and the bed linens had left marks on his right cheek. He sleeps on his stomach or side, she thought, then wrenched her mind from such a bent. From the corner of her eye, she watched him tighten the belt of his gray bathrobe. He was barefoot... bare everything under that robe? She steeled her mind against those thoughts again.

"Don't you have to go on a long trail ride in a few hours?" he asked.

"No, it's been rescheduled because of the rain."

"Rain?" He glanced at her raincoat and galoshes, then went to the window and looked out. "It wasn't raining when I went to bed."

She laughed incredulously. "It's been raining since eleven. Boy, nothing gets in the way of your beauty sleep, does it?"

"There are many ways to deal with stress," he said, turning slowly from the window to face her. "I sleep the sleep of the dead when I've got problems I can't handle. When I awake I'm stronger and can deal with them."

She shook her head, and her laughter had a tragic ring to it. "Problems. Yes, you certainly dumped them on me tonight."

"Banner, I didn't—"

"It was a sucker punch, Yuri," she interrupted, her hands moving to her midsection. "I didn't see it coming and it knocked me for a loop. Now that I've got my breath and my senses again, I have a few questions I'd like answered."

"Now?"

"Right now." She took off her coat and sat on the couch to remove her wet shoes. "I want to get this behind me so that I can stop thinking about it."

He rubbed his hands up and down his face briskly. "I wish you had room service. I'd love a cup of tea to clear my head. I'm not prepared for this interrogation."

"You're such a helpless baby!" Her tone was sharper than she'd intended, but she wasn't in the mood to be apologetic or charitable. She stood up and crossed the room to a low cabinet. Flinging open its doors, she removed a hot pot, tea bags, creamer and sugar. "Even *I* can heat water!" She took the pot to the sink to fill it, then plugged it in. Picking up two tea bags, she held them by their strings and let them swing in front of her nose. "See these? When the water is hot, you dunk them in it and—miracle of miracles!—you get tea!"

Yuri fell onto the couch, flinging his arms along the back of it and fixing her with a hard glare. "You're charming at three o'clock in the morning. Charming like a snake."

"A snake?" She tossed the tea bags on top of the cabinet. "If there's a snake in the grass around here, it's you."

"I'm not going to spar with you." He reached down and pulled the robe together where it had inched apart to expose his muscled thighs. "Let's get this game of twenty questions over with."

"Yes, let's." She eased herself into one of the chairs and tucked her feet under her to warm them. "Did you meet my mother?"

"No. Your mother and my father were dead by the time I defected." He yawned, hiding it behind one hand. "You could have figured that out by yourself."

"I don't know which things you've lied about and which things you haven't. As far as I know, you might have lived here all your life."

"I'm not a habitual liar. Everything I told you was true except my last name." He rubbed his eyes gingerly. "Is that water hot yet?"

"Is your leg broken?" she shot back. "I'm not your maid."

"Okay, okay!" He pushed himself up and went to the cabinet. "I'm trying to be civil, Banner, but you're trying my patience. I'll answer your questions, but I won't tolerate your venom."

"I have a right to be venomous. I'm the wronged party here, not you."

"Do you want some tea?" he asked behind her.

"Yes, please." She lifted her hand to receive the cup when he paused beside her chair. He walked past her to the couch, leaving her hand suspended in the air, and Banner realized she'd been had.

"Then get it yourself, *dear*." His smile was chilling. "See? It's not fun on the receiving end, is it?"

She shrugged off his childish prank. "I don't want any tea."

"Too lazy to get it yourself?"

"I just don't want any!"

He winced at her shrill voice and held up a placating hand. "Now who's broadcasting?" One corner of his mouth twitched into a grin. "You thought I'd been lying about my bachelorhood. I wish it had been that simple."

"Me, too. I could have handled that."

"You can handle this, too." His gaze met hers over the rim of the tea cup. "It's not that terrible, is it? I won't hold your being Diana's daughter against you if you won't hold my being Vladimir's son against me."

"Why did you come here and open up this can of worms?" she asked, her voice suddenly weary and void of sarcasm. "What purpose did it serve?"

"I wanted to meet you. I had two weeks of vacation with nothing to do, and I kept thinking about you—what you were like, what you looked like, how you'd turned out. Didn't you ever wonder about his children?"

"No. Well..." She shrugged, realizing that she had thought about them from time to time. "I used to wonder how his family had taken it. I'd heard that he had several children."

"Four. I have two younger brothers and one younger sister. My sister is married, but my brothers aren't." He frowned and gazed moodily into the cup. "That is, they weren't when I left. Boris might be married by now. He was seeing a lot of a young woman...." He sighed wistfully. "I hear no news from them. We heard nothing about my father, either, except that he'd taken an American mistress. Bad news is leaked."

"Did they notify you when he died?"

"No. I didn't know about that until after I arrived here."

"How did your mother take the news about his mistress?"

He set the cup on the coffee table and seemed to choose his words carefully. "My mother is a fortress of strength. She thrives on sorrow."

"Like a martyr?"

...be tempted!

See inside for special
4 FREE BOOKS offer

Silhouette Desire®

Discover deliciously different Romance with 4 Free Novels from

Silhouette Desire®

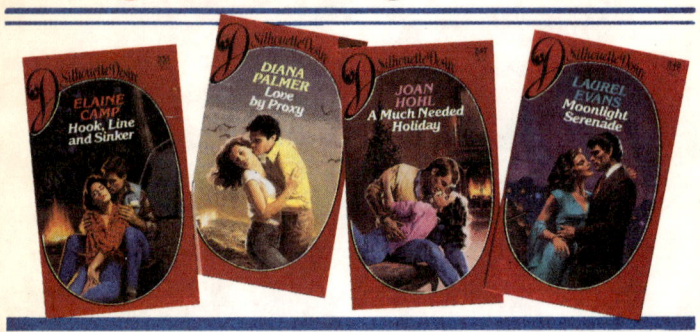

...be enchanted!

As a Silhouette home subscriber, the enchantment begins with Elaine Camp's HOOK, LINE AND SINKER, the story of a woman who must overcome a lie to make real romance possible...Diane Palmer's LOVE BY PROXY, her startling beauty convinced him she was the woman he wanted—on his own terms...Joan Hohl's A MUCH NEEDED HOLIDAY, what begins as a contest of wills turns into an all-consuming passion Kate cannot seem to control...and Laurel Evans' MOONLIGHT SERENADE, the story of a woman who enjoyed her life in the slow lane —until she met the handsome New York TV producer.

...be our guest!

These exciting, love-filled, full-length novels are yours *absolutely FREE along with your Folding Umbrella and Mystery Gift*...a present from us to you. They're yours to keep no matter what you decide.

...be delighted!

After you receive your 4 FREE books, we'll send you 6 more Silhouette Desire novels each and every month to examine FREE for 15 days. If you decide to keep them, pay just $11.70 (a $13.50 value)— with no additional charges for home delivery! If you aren't completely delighted, just drop us a note and we'll cancel your subscription, no questions asked.

EXTRA BONUS: You'll also receive the Silhouette Books Newsletter FREE with each book shipment. Every issue is filled with interviews, news about upcoming books, recipes from your favorite authors, and more.

To get your 4 FREE novels, Folding Umbrella, and Mystery Gift, just fill out and mail the attached order card. Remember, the first 4 novels and both gifts are yours to keep. Are you ready to be tempted?

A FREE
Folding Umbrella
and Mystery Gift
await you, too!

← *Clip and mail this postpaid card today!* ↙

NO POSTAGE NECESSARY IF MAILED IN THE UNITED STATES

BUSINESS REPLY MAIL
FIRST CLASS PERMIT NO. 194 CLIFTON, N.J.

Postage will be paid by addressee
**Silhouette Books
120 Brighton Road
P.O. Box 5084
Clifton, NJ 07015-9956**

Mail this card today for

4 FREE BOOKS
(a $9.00 value)
this Folding Umbrella and
a Mystery Gift ALL FREE!

← Clip and mail this postpaid card today! →

☐ **YES!** Please send me my four Silhouette Desire novels along with my FREE Folding Umbrella and Mystery Gift, as explained in this insert. I understand that I am under no obligation to purchase any books.

Silhouette Desire®

Silhouette Books, 120 Brighton Rd., P.O. Box 5084, Clifton, NJ 07015-9956

NAME _____ (please print)

ADDRESS _____

CITY _____ STATE _____ ZIP _____

Terms and prices subject to change.
Your enrollment is subject to acceptance by Silhouette Books.

Silhouette Desire is a registered trademark.

CAD086

He nodded, smiling wryly. "Exactly. My mother the martyr."

"I didn't mean that to sound so... I wasn't criticizing."

"I know, but your description is precise. I don't blame her, but I wish she'd shared some of her insight with us. She kept us in the dark and things are distorted in the dark."

"I'm not quite sure what you're getting at," Banner confessed, trying to read something in his gloomy expression. "Are you saying that she knew things about your father that she kept to herself?"

"Yes." He stood up and went to fill his tea cup again. He brought a cup to her this time, smiling apologetically when he handed it to her, then resuming his place on the couch. "She knew the circumstances of his defection, but she never told us about them. She let us think that Vladimir deserted us with no regard to our welfare."

"Didn't he?"

"Not entirely." He sipped the tea thoughtfully, and the sound of the rain filled the quiet room. "Sometimes it's easier to think the worst of people, Banner, but it's not fair. It's just easier."

"Is this the beginning of a lecture? Because if it is—"

"No, I won't lecture you." He cleared his throat. "Next question, please."

"How did you know where to find me?"

He swallowed a mouthful of tea with a gulp and laughed. "It didn't take much investigation. You've lived here all your life."

"What did you hope to accomplish?"

"Nothing, really. I have a keen curiosity." He smiled briefly. "A prerequisite for an engineer. My motives were ambivalent. I certainly didn't come here to harm you. I merely thought that you and I had a common bond. After I met you, I sensed your bitterness and I thought I might be able to help. I was bitter once, but not anymore."

"Goody for you." Her sarcasm brought another frown to his face, but she didn't care. She hated his holier-than-thou attitude. He didn't know what she'd been through. Her situation was different. His parents had been separated by land and water, unable to reach each other again. All her mother had to do was come back to Oklahoma and all would have been forgiven. She and her father could have patched things up. Diana hadn't been willing to make that concession.

"You're determined not to forgive and forget, aren't you?" he asked.

"I *had* forgotten until you stirred it up again!"

His smile was derisive. "I don't believe that, so I'm sure you don't, either. The moment you realized I was Russian you treated me as if I had the black plague!"

"I didn't!"

"You did. You *know* you did!"

"Your being Russian had nothing to do with it! I didn't like your attitude. You were rude and obnoxious."

"Oh, hell!" He shot up from the couch and strode to the window. "I saw the hatred in your eyes when I told you I was Russian! I heard the contempt in your voice when you spoke about the Soviet Union! I would have confessed sooner about my identity if it hadn't been for your blind prejudice."

She twisted around in the chair to look at him. Half of his face was illuminated by the lamp's glow. His morning beard was heavy, darkening his cheeks and jaw. His ebony hair was ruffled, falling jaggedly across his forehead and over the tops of his ears. His wide, full mouth dipped at the corners as he stared at the rain-splattered windowpane. Dark Russian, she thought. Dark, moody Russian. Memories of his mouth on hers came to her unbidden, unwanted. There was so much passion within him, she thought. She had experienced it, shared it, reveled in it. Never had she met a man with such intense passion—not just sexual, but emotional and spiritual.

"You look so very much like her," he murmured, then looked at her from the corner of his eyes. "Did you know that?" He laughed softly when she turned her face from him. "Sorry if that offends you, but it's true. Right down to that birthmark on your left cheek. The resemblance is startling."

"And that's where the resemblance ends," she assured him. "I'm not like her in any other way." She gasped, seizing on his revelation. "You've seen her? Pictures of her?"

"Yes, a few. She was famous. Haven't you seen photos of my father?"

"Only one, and that was by accident." She remembered the photo of a tall, lithe man with a mane of white hair and dark, flashing eyes. He'd had a noble nose, wide mouth, a brooding cast to his face. Banner stared at Yuri as her mind fit that picture over his face for a clear comparison. "You...you resemble him," she whispered with a touch of awe. "The same mouth, nose, eyes. His hair was white, but—"

"Give me a few years," Yuri said, chuckling under his breath as he lifted a hand to touch the silver hair at his temples. "I'm getting there."

She nodded, imagining him with silvery hair instead of ebony. Yes, just like Vladimir. "Are you musically inclined?"

"No, my younger brother, Illya, inherited all of my father's musical talent. When my father was with us our home was filled with music, but after he left the music died." He leaned a shoulder against the window frame and his voice grew soft and raspy. "I was glad when Illya showed an interest in music and brought it back into our lives. My father could play several instruments, but he was adept at the violin. Illya's a demon on the piano. He's only eighteen, but he's composed two sonatas and a waltz. My father would be proud of him."

"You're proud of him," Banner said, smiling at the tenderness he'd displayed.

"Yes, very proud."

His smile warmed her, making her feel that spark of love again. She averted her gaze, unable to cope with such sentiment.

"How much do you know about Vladimir and Diana?" she asked, staring blindly at the painting above the couch.

"Everything."

She turned her head slowly toward him, her blue eyes wide and searching. "Everything?"

"Yes, I believe so."

Banner swallowed with difficulty. Her mouth had become dry, and she took a sip of tea and laid the cup down before she tried to speak again. "But, how? How could you know?"

"I have my father's diary." He nodded when she made a sound of disbelief. "Yes, it's true. It seems that Vladimir was not only a writer of music, but of feelings, emotions, secrets of the heart." He moved closer and placed a hand on her shoulder. His gaze held hers in a gentle embrace. "You were right about Diana. She was a woman who was hard to forget. Just as your father was obsessed with her, so was mine." He bent at the waist until his eyes were level with hers. "And, Banner, how I envy my father. His love for her was what love should be—all consuming and eternal. I want that kind of love. We all do."

She inched back, wary of him. "Not me. Theirs was a selfish love. A destructive force. I want no part of it."

"You're wrong, Banner."

"Don't lecture me!" She pushed him aside and stood up angrily. "I'm a casualty of their love and so are you!"

"Running away from the truth again?"

She hadn't realized that she had moved to the front door until he spoke, then she looked at her hand resting on the knob and slumped wearily against the door.

"No. I guess it's too late to run," she whispered, then laughed when she saw her bare feet. "Especially like this." She sat on the couch and pulled on the galoshes again. "I'm tired. I can't discuss this right now." She straightened and looked toward the bedroom, then went across the room to it. She peeked inside at the disheveled bed, illuminated by the bedside lamp, then her gaze moved to the closet. As she'd expected, it was empty. Two suitcases sat on the floor.

"See something that interests you?" Yuri asked.

"I thought you might have packed your things," she said, looking at him, then reaching for her coat and slipping into it with his help. His hands brushed her shoulders ever so slightly after her coat was on and she looked back at him, suddenly unwilling to say goodbye. "Don't leave."

"You want me to stay after—"

"Yes." She pulled her coat tighter around her. "If I can't run away, then neither can you. It's only fair, right?"

He smiled and nodded. "Only fair."

"Good, then I'll see you later this morning. Get some sleep. You'll need it." She went to the front door and opened it. The wind blew raindrops into her face and tossed her dark hair. She smiled and glanced at him. "Do you think we can weather this storm, Yuri?" she asked, then closed the door behind her before he could answer.

Six

"Aren't you coming in for dinner?" DiDi asked when Banner lingered near Honey's stall.

"No, you go on." Banner stroked the palomino's white mane, then leaned her forehead against Honey's neck. "I'm skipping dinner." She turned her head to see DiDi's concerned expression. "This rain has made me melancholy."

"I know what you mean," DiDi said, glancing in the direction of the guests who were hurrying toward the main house to escape the misty rain. "But tomorrow should be better. The stables are cold. You shouldn't stay out here too long." Turning back to Banner, DiDi rested a hand on her arm. "Want to talk about whatever's bothering you?"

Banner placed a hand on DiDi's. "It's hard to put into words. I just need time to think some things through."

"Does this have anything to do with Yuri?"

"Yes, but not entirely," Banner admitted. "How did you know that?"

"I haven't seen him all day. I called his cabin to remind him of the farrier demonstration, but he said he wasn't interested."

"That shouldn't surprise you. He's not interested in anything around here. Hadn't you noticed?"

DiDi tucked her hands into the pockets of her red slicker and winked. "I noticed that he's interested in you and that you're interested in him. Is that what you want to think through?"

"That's part of it." Banner combed her fingers through Honey's forelock, stalling as she searched for the right words to convey her quandary. She could talk to DiDi, she told herself. She and DiDi had been close friends for years. If anyone would understand her mixed feelings for the ranch and the Russian it would be DiDi. "You know that I love the ranch, that it's been my cornerstone all my life."

"Sure. Never a doubt."

"Then why have I been so restless lately?" Banner asked, turning toward DiDi. She massaged the back of her neck, kneading the knots of tension there. "Ever since Dad died things haven't been the same. I'm not completely satisfied." She moaned and closed her eyes. "What's wrong with me?"

"Banner, nothing's wrong with you. Look, I love pumpkin pie better than anything, but I don't want a steady diet of it! I worship Pete, but I don't want to spend every waking moment with him." She placed her hands on Banner's shoulders and concern lined her freckled face. "Hon, I don't know how you've stayed here day in, day out. I swear, I've wondered what keeps you tied to this piece of land. This ranch is important to you, but it can't give you everything. I'll tell you one thing, if I hadn't found Pete here I wouldn't be staying around."

"You wouldn't?"

"No way." DiDi laughed, bringing an uncertain smile to Banner's lips. "Don't torture yourself because you've got itchy feet. You know that me and Pete can run things if you want to get away for a while."

Banner sighed wearily. "I don't know what I want." She looked around the stables, remembering times she had spent here with her father. "This place holds all my memories. Dad loved the ranch. It was enough for him."

"You're his daughter, not his twin."

"I'm her daughter, too," Banner whispered, then moved away from DiDi. "It wasn't enough for her. Am I like her?"

"What if you are?" DiDi moved swiftly to step in front of Banner. "She wasn't so bad. She was a talented, ambitious woman. Besides, you're talking nonsense. Your mother chose not to come back, but that doesn't mean you're going to make the same choice." DiDi gripped Banner's upper arms and shook her. "I know what you're thinking. You're thinking about Yuri being Russian and how your mother took off with a Russian. Banner, that's just a silly coincidence. You hear me? Don't draw comparisons where there aren't any."

"You don't understand," Banner said.

"Yes, I do. That Russian likes you and you're keeping him at arm's length because of something he had nothing to do with!"

Banner smiled sadly at DiDi, appreciating her attempts to make her see reason where there wasn't any. Who could make sense of this mess? She felt as if she were living someone else's life—Diana's life.

"He's Vladimir's son," Banner said, only realizing that she'd spoken when DiDi gasped.

"What put that idea in your head?" DiDi asked, laughing a little. "You're all confused."

"Don't I wish!" Banner shook her head, dispelling DiDi's theory. "He told me last night. His last name isn't Mytova. It's Zaarbo."

DiDi covered her mouth with her hands, and her eyes widened to bright, glazed orbs. She took a wobbly step back as if the news had knocked her off balance.

"He t-told you that?" DiDi asked, then let her hands slip from her lips. "Did he know who you were when he came here?"

"Yes, that's why he's here. He wanted to meet Diana's daughter."

"Holy smoke!" DiDi ran a hand through her red curls in a distracted gesture. "This is too weird!"

"Tell me about it." Banner sat down on a bale of hay and smiled at DiDi's pale face. "You're taking the news better than I did." She laughed and patted the hay next to her. "Better sit down before you fall down."

DiDi sat down heavily. "No wonder you're in such a stupor. Can I do anything to help?"

"Like what? Can you wave a magic wand and make him disappear?"

"Is that what you want?"

Banner considered the question for a few moments, then shrugged helplessly. "No. That wouldn't solve anything." She glanced sideways at DiDi and lowered her voice to a more private pitch. "There's something about him, DiDi. I've never... well, he's a fascinating man."

"In other words, you're sweet on him."

Banner laughed at the quaint phrase and placed an arm around DiDi's shoulders. "Let's just say that I'm attracted to him—against my better judgment. It's strange, but from the first moment I saw him I knew he was different. I couldn't put my finger on it, but I was drawn to him. Even when I was so mad at him that I wanted to kick him from here to Tulsa, there was a part of me that still liked him."

"I'm surprised you don't hate him for lying to you." DiDi frowned and plucked a piece of straw from the hay. "I would. Why didn't he tell you right off who he was?"

"He sensed my grudge against Russians."

DiDi gave her a sidelong glance. "He didn't need ESP for that." She grinned, taking the edge off her words. "But he should have told you right off that he was Vladimir's son. Is he checking out? Is that why he didn't show his face today?"

"No, I asked him to stay." She caught DiDi's appraising glance. "Don't jump to conclusions," Banner warned. "I'm not sure why I asked him to stay. It was the middle of the night and I'm not the type to turn my guests away. Besides, he seems to know a lot about Diana."

"You never wanted to know anything about her, did you?"

"No, and I'm not sure I want to know now." She smiled at the irony. "Like I said before, I don't know what I want. Everything used to be so simple. I hate to be in limbo, unable to know who I am or what I want or which way to turn."

"It's not that bad," DiDi reassured her. "We all go through times of indecision. Things will work out. You'll find the right path to take."

"I hope so." Banner stood up with DiDi. "Cover for me at dinner, okay? I'm just not in the hostess mood this evening."

"Sure, I understand." DiDi tapped a finger under Banner's chin. "Chin up. The sun will shine tomorrow and everything will look brighter."

"That's what Dad always said when I had the blues." She sighed and glanced up at the rough beams. "I miss him. While he was here I had a purpose."

"You still do." DiDi flipped up the hood of her rain jacket and tucked her red hair under it. "You really like Yuri, huh?"

"He's okay."

"Ha!" DiDi wagged a finger at her. "I know you too well, Banner O'Bryan. That man has found places in your heart you didn't even know were there!"

Banner stared after DiDi, watching as she dodged puddles and mud holes on her way to the house. Leave it to DiDi to make things crystal clear, Banner thought with respect. She was right. Yuri Myto—Zaarbo had broken through her icy shell. She'd tried to keep him out, but he'd barged right in and staked a claim on her.

Walking slowly to the other end of the stables, Banner was barely aware of the shuffle of hooves on hay and the soft nickers of the horses she passed. The open-ended stables allowed the wind to tunnel through, and the air was chilly and damp. Banner buttoned her leather jacket and examined the watery vista before her. Mist clung to trees and fell in drops to the saturated ground.

Rainy days were difficult at the ranch. Indoor activities had to be planned for the guests. The staff was called on to entertain and keep everyone's mind off the gray weather. Since the rain wasn't supposed to let up until after midnight, Banner had hired a band to entertain the guests after dinner at the Shortbranch. She'd engaged a troupe of square dancers, too. It would be a festive evening despite the rain.

Any other time she'd be looking forward to it, but she wasn't sure if she could drag herself to the dance. The day had been draining enough. She'd put on a happy face during breakfast, a quilting lesson conducted by DiDi and the farrier's lesson on horseshoeing, all the while wishing she could curl into a corner with her thoughts and sort things out for herself.

Is that what Yuri had done all day?

She lifted her gaze to watch a flock of blackbirds sail overhead, and she yearned to go with them. It would be lovely to spread her wings and soar above her small, cloistered world.

The ranch had always been enough for her, so why wasn't it enough now? Lately, she had found herself thinking about other careers, other choices. She remembered how hard it had been to leave Oklahoma City and come back to the ranch. She had wanted to continue with her schooling. While her classmates had groaned over math problems, Banner had been absorbed with them. She'd taken an aptitude test and had been at the top of her class in mathematics. Her instructor had encouraged her to continue her studies, pointing out all the careers that would open up once she had a degree. Accounting, bookkeeping, executive secretary, science, computers, research, engineering. It had all sounded exciting, but Banner had known that Luke was waiting for her to return, and she hadn't the heart to disappoint him.

She remembered how happy Luke had been when she'd come back home. He'd said that he'd been afraid she might decide to stay in Oklahoma City, but Banner had told him that she had missed the ranch.

"Well, you never know," Luke had said, rubbing his jaw thoughtfully. "The big city has a way of catching you and keeping you."

"Not me," Banner had said, wanting him to believe in her and her devotion to him. "I'm a country girl and always will be."

That had been a white lie, she thought. She'd liked living in the city. Yes, she'd missed the ranch and her father, but she had enjoyed the change of pace and scenery. She wouldn't have stayed away from the ranch no matter what. Luke had loved her and made a good home for her, and she wouldn't desert him. She couldn't bear the thought of his being alone.

Alone. She was the one who'd been left alone. She closed her eyes and swallowed hard. Funny how you could be surrounded by people all the time and still feel alone. Yuri had made her achingly aware of that. When she was with him, she hardly recognized herself. Feelings erupted, passions flowered, time stood still. It confused her, frightened her, tempted her. How could she live twenty-six years and not know her every emotion, her every reaction? Yet, when she was in Yuri's arms she was floating on a river of surprise and adventure, not knowing what would be around the next bend or if she would sink or swim.

Every time she closed her eyes, she thought of him. Even now she could see the sunlight in his hair, the dark intrigue of his eyes and masculine grace of his body. She could hear his voice, low timbred and lightly accented, familiar and unfamiliar, friendly and foreign. His smile haunted her, beckoning her to unknown heights and spine-tingling desire. He was the serpent in the garden, and she was the innocent, titillated Eve.

What scared her was that she liked the way he made her feel. She liked to touch him and to be touched by him. She liked the flirtation of his mouth on hers. She liked everything about him... except his last name and what it meant. Zaarbo. Like Shakespeare's Juliet she wondered what was in a name. If a rose were called by any other name would it not smell as sweet? If Yuri weren't a Zaarbo would she find him more attractive? She shook her head, smiling faintly, then she heard a light footfall and knew it was Yuri before he spoke.

"I thought I might find you here," he said, his voice growing stronger as he moved closer to her.

"Why aren't you at dinner? Are you skipping it, too?" she asked, opening her eyes to the gray day again.

"I lost my appetite when I saw that you weren't at the table." He stopped beside her and leaned forward to peer into her face. Raindrops clung to his long lashes and heavy brows. His hair was a dark, wet cap. "Are we speaking to each other?"

"Looks that way." She hugged herself, warding off the chilly breeze and the nearness of him. "There's a square dance tonight."

"So I heard. Will you be there?"

"I'm not sure."

"Please be there. It will be good for both of us to mingle with the others and relieve some of the tension we've created."

"You've created," she corrected, then wished she'd kept her snappy reply to herself. He sighed heavily and tucked his hands high up under his arms to keep them warm.

His red plaid shirt was damp, and Banner breathed in the scent of wet wool and a fading trace of after-shave. She glanced down at his muddy boots and splattered jeans. How could a mud-splashed man be so attractive? she wondered.

"If it will make things better between us, I'll be more than happy to take all the blame." He shivered and stepped back. "That breeze is wicked. Aren't you freezing?"

"No," she lied. "I came here to be alone."

"And I'm intruding," he finished for her. "Last night was so...so chaotic, I just thought you might want to talk now."

"What's there to talk about?"

"About Diana and my father."

"Why would I want to talk about them?" she asked, looking directly at him.

"Well, last night...rather, this morning...you implied—"

"I was confused, stunned. I didn't know what to think. But I don't want to know anything about Diana. I know enough. And I certainly don't give a damn about your father!"

He stared at her unflinchingly, but she sensed his temper and saw it blaze in his eyes like a flash of lightning. "You know nothing, but I can see that you're quite happy with that."

"I told you that I don't want to be lectured."

"What do you want, Banner? I was going to leave, but you asked me to stay. Why?"

"I wasn't thinking clearly." She wasn't thinking clearly now, either, she thought. Why was it that when he was near she was a mass of contradictions? Wanting, not wanting; believing, not believing; angry, not angry.

"Do you want me to leave now? Is that what you're saying?"

"Do whatever you want!" She stared blindly at the soggy scenery and wished she could make sense.

"I want to take you to the square dance tonight," he said, moving closer until his body brushed against hers.

"I haven't decided to go."

"Then I'll meet you there."

"You are the most persistent, pigheaded man I've ever met!"

"Pigheaded?" He mulled over the expression for a moment. "Now that's one I haven't heard. Does it mean that I'm stupid or ugly?"

She tried to keep the smile from her face, but failed. Laughing under her breath, she glanced at him and was struck by his darkly brooding face. Just like Vladimir, she thought. Dark, sensuous, dangerously attractive.

"You're not stupid or ugly," she said, looking away from his soulful eyes. "I meant that your stubborn streak is showing."

"I don't know about you, but I've spent the day in misery and I'd enjoy an evening away from it. Square dancing isn't on my list of favorite things, but beggars can't be choosers. Meet me tonight, Banner. I don't know why you asked me to stay, but I know why I took you up on the offer. I want to be with you."

Her throat constricted and she wanted to echo his thoughts, but she couldn't find the courage. Instead, she looked at him and laid a hand on his damp sleeve. The gesture pleased him, and he covered her hand with his.

"That's a beginning. You don't mind if I take this as a sign of encouragement?"

His fingers moved across the back of her hand before he stepped out of her reach and into the cold rain. He stood facing her, oblivious to the downpour.

"I'll be at the dance by eight," he said, his gaze never wavering from the brilliant blue of her eyes. "Don't stand me up. Don't let the past ruin our friendship. We were friends, weren't we?"

"Yes." She waved her hands, shooing him away. "Go on. You're getting soaked!"

"I'll see you tonight?"

"Yes, yes. Will you please go? You'll catch a cold!"

"Tonight, Banner." He turned up the collar of his shirt, then whirled around and ran through the rain, leaping over puddles and sliding on the wet grass. She watched until she could no longer see him through the fog that had rolled in from the foothills.

He didn't know why she'd asked him to stay, but she knew. It was clear to her now. She'd asked him to stay because she couldn't bear to say goodbye to him. Even after she'd learned that he was Vladimir's son, she hadn't been able to order him from her life.

Banner shivered, but not from the chilly breeze. Her eyes widened as a feeling deep within her evolved into a clear, concise thought. She was falling in love with him. He'd been right not to tell her his real name until now. He'd spun a web and she was caught in it. She could still break free, but she wasn't sure she wanted to.

It was almost eight o'clock when Banner entered the Shortbranch. She stood just inside the doors for a few moments to get her bearings. The band was playing at full steam, and the Rocking Horse guests were watching the Calico Square Dancers whirl to the commands of the caller. The women's full skirts lifted to show off layers of stiff petticoats. The men wore boots, jeans, checked shirts and string ties. The click of boot heels sounded on the wood floor along with the tap of flat, T-strap shoes.

Banner had chosen an ivory dress with a midlength circle skirt and tight, vested waist. Her doeskin boots were off-white, more urban than Western. She knew she looked as elegant as a string of pearls, but inside she was all paste. She was at a fever pitch of excitement, complete with sweaty palms, frayed nerves and pounding heart. This was as close to a date as she'd had in months. It had been a long dry spell and she was thirsty for romance.

She'd decided to pull out all stops and make the most of the situation. Yuri had practically begged her to meet him, and she'd decided not to disappoint him. She'd chosen her outfit carefully and with great calculation, spinning a web all her own. No more shying away from him like a scared filly, she'd told herself firmly. She was a woman. He was a man. They shared an attraction. For tonight, she was bound and determined to keep within those confines and not to allow the shadow of Diana and Vladimir to encroach on her boundaries.

She scanned the room for that smile that would be all hers, that certain look meant just for her. She'd gone to great lengths to look beautiful, and she wanted her reward.

"Oh, there she is," Flo Ferguson said to her husband, looking toward the bat-wing doors. "Isn't she lovely tonight?"

Yuri swiveled around on the bar stool, knowing it was Banner that Flo was pointing out. The Fergusons had been wondering aloud if their hostess would show up for the dance, since she had missed dinner. She was here at last, Yuri thought as his gaze swung to the doors and zeroed in on the vision in ivory. His breathing stilled for a few moments, and his chest tightened with an attraction so intense, so consuming that he felt light-headed. His heart kicked against his ribs, and he realized that he had risen to his feet without being conscious of moving.

How could flesh and blood seem so ethereal? She was like a painting, a photograph, a treasured dream. Not real. Too beautiful to be real. However, when he stood before her and lightly held her hands in his, she was warm and alive. A fantasy come to life.

"Banner Bright, Banner Bright," he heard himself chanting, "Oh, what a vision you are tonight."

There was a brief glimpse of wariness in her eyes, but it melted into a glimmer of appreciation.

"Why, Yuri, I had no idea you were a poet." She laughed, low and huskily, and her cheeks flushed with embarrassment.

She couldn't think of anything else to say. His smile spoke fathoms to her, making her feel far more beautiful than she'd ever felt before. He had dressed in gray: dark gray slacks and a charcoal gray sweater. Somber colors to enhance his brooding personality.

Opposites, Banner thought. We're opposites. He's night and I'm day. He's the moon and I'm the sun. Separate, but counterbalancing each other.

"One needs only inspiration to find poetry, and you've inspired me," he said, then lifted one of her hands and kissed the back of it. His gaze moved over her hair. "Has it stopped raining?"

"It stopped raining just as I was leaving the house." She smiled and removed her hands from his. "Perfect timing."

She looked around, suddenly feeling conspicuous. The last thing she wanted was for her guests to notice how absorbed she was by Yuri. If they saw her blushing or heard the breathless quality in her voice they'd know that Yuri was more to her than just a paying customer. She wanted to keep this private. His hand pressed against the small of her back, and he guided her to a table for two. She was amused by her own reaction to his slightest touch. It warmed her through and through. She smiled across the table at him, and he moved his chair closer to hers.

"You take my breath away," he said, speaking in a whisper. "I feel like a sprig of ragweed next to a white rose." He lifted one hand to summon the waitress. "What will you have to drink?"

"A brandy, please."

"And I'll have another beer, please," he told the waitress, then swung his attention back to Banner. "I'd ask you to dance, but I refuse to make a fool of myself out there by attempting to square dance."

"It isn't as hard as it looks."

"It reminds me of some folk dances I learned as a boy." He watched the dancers, laughing when some of the novices made a wrong turn and added more confusion to the scene. "I think I'll pass." He curved one arm behind her back. "I suppose you've been thinking about Vladimir and Diana."

"I don't want to talk about them," she said quickly, wanting to stop the conversation before it could begin. "I've decided that the less I know the better off I'll be. Let's forget them."

"Ignorance is bliss." A sardonic smile curved his lips. "She was your mother, and you don't know anything about her."

"And you do?" she asked, irritated by his insistence to dwell on unhappy things.

"More than you," he shot back, then grew silent while the waitress set their drinks on the table.

After the waitress left the table, Banner leaned closer to Yuri and lowered her voice to a whisper.

"For the life of me, I don't see how you can be the least bit interested in them. Your father deserted you and your family!"

"He didn't desert me," Yuri corrected patiently. "He left Russia. For the life of me, I don't understand why you insist on holding onto your canards!"

"My...canards?" Banner racked her brain, searching for the elusive meaning of that word, then sighing with relief when she found it. "Lies, you mean?" She caught his smile and sent it back. "There's nothing more irritating than a foreigner who knows English better than a native."

"We're even," he told her. "You had to explain 'pigheaded' to me." He held up his stein of beer and tapped it against her brandy snifter. "To bright beginnings."

She took a sip of the brandy, felt it burn and add fuel to her curiosity. So much for closing the lid on Vladimir and Diana. Yuri had opened Pandora's box and let them out again. "Why did your father feel that he had to leave his family and country?"

"His reasons were astonishingly similar to mine." Yuri relaxed in the chair and his hand moved up to her shoulder. "That's what surprised me the most...the similarities between him and myself. He was vocally critical of the restrictions on art in Russia. Finally, the government took steps to teach him a lesson on keeping his opinions to himself. He was removed from his conductor's podium and told that he would spend the next five years teaching music to students. Of course, he couldn't stand for that. An artist as great as my father can't abide repression." He paused to gather his thoughts and noticed that Banner was looking off to one side, her face set in grave lines as if she were enduring pain. "You can't even stand to hear his name mentioned, can you?"

Banner swung her attention back to him, realizing that he'd read her mind with ease. She shook her head apologetically, but couldn't make herself speak the appropriate words.

"Yuri, I've hated that man ever since I was ten. I can't change my feelings for him overnight. I'm glad you respect him, but I can't. Can't we please talk about something else? I'd hoped that we could get to know each other instead of rehashing Vladimir and Diana and their affair."

"Your mother didn't leave because of my father. She met him *after* she left your father."

"That's Vladimir's version of the story, isn't it?"

"That's the truth, Banner."

"No." Banner tipped up her chin, refusing to cave in. "She left for someone."

"She left for some*thing*."

Banner stood up, her lips set in a grim line. "Let's dance."

"Banner, listen—"

"No." She flashed him a warning glance. "I don't want to dredge it up again. Now are you going to dance or am I going to have to find a willing partner?"

"Are you sure you want to dance with Vladimir's son?"

She flinched and wished he hadn't phrased it that way. "Don't push your luck," she said, reaching for his hand as he stood up. "I came here to have fun, not to fight. What about you?"

His hand curled around hers, and he slipped his other arm around her waist. "I'll join you only because they've stopped square dancing. Well, that's not entirely true." He brushed his lips across her forehead. "Any excuse to hold you in my arms is fine with me."

"You're just full of pretty words tonight, aren't you? Are you trying to impress me?"

"I think I've already made an impression on you." He smiled and kissed the tip of her nose. "But I'm not sure if it's a good or bad impression."

"Both." She looked down at his black boots, realizing that he was dancing with a grace that was rare in a man. The band was playing a slow, bluesy tune for a change of pace from the lively square dancing. She eyed him speculatively, noting his light tread and sure steps.

"Did you, by chance, take dancing lessons?"

"Yes, in Moscow. It's not so unusual there for a young boy to receive training in ballet."

"Ballet?" She couldn't picture him in tights. "I was thinking more in the vein of ballroom dancing."

"Oh, no." He pulled her closer, erasing the buffer of space she'd relied on. "Once you learn the basics of ballet, all forms of dance are easily learned."

Banner rested her free hand against his chest and tipped up her chin to look at him. "I'm surprised that you learned to dance. It has nothing to do with the work ethic."

He looked over the top of her head and smiled. "It really bothers you that I love my work, doesn't it?"

"No, it bothers me that you love it to an extreme."

"I love other things, too."

"Oh, like what?"

"Sunsets and fireplaces," he whispered, still looking past her as he compiled his list. "Sunday mornings and fresh coffee. Family gatherings and newborn babies." His gaze lowered to hers. "Blue eyes and beauty marks." He dipped his head, and his lips grazed the mark on her cheek, then traveled lightly to her mouth.

His effect on her senses was immediate, sending a wave of longing through her. She pressed her palm flat against his chest and felt the beating of his heart.

Here you go again, falling, falling, falling under his spell, an inner voice chided.

He had weakened her defenses to such a degree that they were flimsy. He had made her taste the wine of desire and she'd become addicted. He had offered her something different and she had grabbed it. She remembered the first time he'd kissed her and how frightened she'd been of her feelings for him. That kiss had sealed her fate. He had said that he'd imprinted himself on her heart and he was right. She'd never forget him, never be free of him.

Her mouth hovered near his, brushing across his lips then waiting for him to imitate and initiate. He didn't kiss her fully, but gave her shadow kisses that were there and gone. His breath warmed her skin as his lips traced the contours of her face with soft strokes, like the caress of a painter's brush across a canvas.

Banner closed her eyes, losing herself in the dance of his mouth. He was an expert at temptation, giving her a sample of what could happen if she wanted to give herself to him.

"Banner Bright," he whispered before his lips shimmied down her throat.

There was a time when she had despised that name and all it conjured up, but when he said it her heart lifted. What's in a name? What's in a name? Banner Bright. Zaarbo. Diana. Just names, her mind chanted as if trying to convince her that this moment was right and ripe with passion.

"Run away with me," he murmured in her ear. "Let me lay the world at your feet. I'll break the chains of boredom and let you soar with only your imagination to limit you."

She smiled and floated with his whispered words. Oh, how lovely it would be to run away with him, she thought.

To escape the confines of this life— Banner stiffened and leaned back in the circle of Yuri's arms. She stared at him, alarmed by the ease of his seduction and her readiness. Like father, like son. Like mother, like daughter.

"Banner? What's wrong?"

"This." She pushed his arms away from her body. "This is wrong." She looked around, feeling dazed and bewildered. "We shouldn't be doing this," she murmured. "We're making a spectacle of ourselves. We're fooling ourselves. Besides, I'm not as easy a mark as my mother."

He stared at her as if she'd lost her mind. "What are you talking about?"

"You asked me to run away with you. Did you think that I was as weak as my mother had been?" She shook her head and backed away from him. "I have responsibilities here. I won't turn my back on them. He said the same things to her, didn't he? He enticed her and she followed him."

"I don't know what he told her. I was talking to you, not your mother!"

Banner squeezed her eyes shut for a few moments and her head swam with visions, real and unreal. Was she making too much of this? Was she seeing a pattern where there wasn't one?

"Come on. Let's go." His hand curved around her elbow, and he guided her from the dance floor. "Will we ever sort this out? Will you ever trust me again?"

"I don't know," she said with a worried glance at him. "Are you sure it's me you like? Sometimes I think that you came here looking for a Diana facsimile."

"Don't be ridiculous!"

They had stepped outside, away from the light and noise. Banner gripped Yuri's forearms and made him look at her.

"Am I being ridiculous?" she charged. "You said that your father wrote of Diana in his diary."

"Yes, that's right."

"Did he write of her beauty? Her talent? Her passionate spirit?"

"Yes." His eyes widened. "So you *do* know something about her!"

"Not really. I just have a notion of how one lover might write of another." She stood on tiptoes and her eyes beseeched his. "Yuri, can you stand there and tell me that you didn't have even the slightest infatuation for Diana Dufrayne?"

He opened his mouth, then paused and shook his head. "No, I can't tell you that."

"So, you see?" She let her hands slip down his muscled arms. "Subconsciously, you probably are more interested in Diana than in me."

"No, I won't agree with that." He stepped off the boardwalk, then turned to face her. "I admit that I was fascinated with what my father wrote about your mother. I told you that I envied their relationship. Their love was so... so binding." He spread out his hands in an appeal. "But I'm not trying to recreate or emulate. How can I relive something that I haven't yet experienced?" He held out his hands, caught hers, and helped her hop from the boardwalk onto the soggy ground. "I came here because I was curious. I admit that. But I don't want Diana. I want you." His teeth flashed in the darkness. "Don't you want me?"

"Yes." Banner sighed with exasperation when he grinned with delight. "Don't look so surprised. I haven't exactly hidden my feelings from you."

"But you keep retreating."

"That's because I don't see any point to this."

"Point?" he echoed. "Since when does sexual attraction have to make a point?"

"I want more than sexual attraction, and I'm not sure I'd find it with you." She removed her hands from his and turned away. The temptation was too great and she didn't trust herself.

"But we have so much in common!"

"You keep saying that, but I don't believe it."

"Banner, Banner, Banner," he chanted like an adult to a child. "Must we go over this again?"

"Over what?"

"What we share besides a healthy desire for each other."

"Be specific," she said, wanting to steer him from that subject.

"We've both been tortured by responsibilities. Some responsibilities are taken and others are given. Those which are taken are easy to manage, but those that are given can be backbreakers." He draped an arm around her shoulders and began walking with her toward the main house. "You understand that, don't you?"

Banner stared at the ground as his message began to make itself clear. "Yes, I suppose.... Are you talking about your decision to leave Russia?"

"Yes. When my father left us I was given the responsibility of being the head of the family. I carried the burden for years, believing that it was my duty to make everyone happy." He sighed and looked up at the glistening tree branches. "But I finally realized that I had a responsibility to myself first and foremost. It's a mistake, I think, to live your life in complete servitude to others."

"You think that's what I've done?"

"It's not important what I think. What do you think? Are you happy, Banner? Has your life gone as you planned or as it was planned for you?"

"I have been happy," she said, more to herself than to him. "I can remember being happy when Dad was here."

"But what about now?"

"I don't know." She stopped and looked around at the landscape that was so much a part of her that she needed no map to see its borders, its trails, its every rise and fall. "This is my heritage... my life."

"This is a *part* of your life, not *all* of it." His free hand smoothed down her cheek in a tingling caress. "When I left Russia I felt as if I were leaving everything I was or had been behind me, but I was wrong." His smile was gentle and full of sentiment. "I took it with me. Russia is in my soul, my memories, my heart. Wherever you go, Banner, your love for this land will go with you."

"Oh, Yuri," she said, sighing as she rested her cheek against his shoulder. "My head is swimming. It does that when I'm with you." She laughed softly along with him. "I spend hours thinking of what you've said and what you haven't said."

"I do the same thing."

"You do?" she asked, lifting her head to look at him.

"Yes. Why don't we stay awake hours together?"

She laughed at the cagey gleam in his eyes and moved away from him. "Not tonight."

"Do I catch a 'maybe later' in that statement?"

She shook her head. "No comment."

"You have a strong will. Stronger than mine." He glanced around, then seized one of her hands and pulled her with him into the deep shadows beside the dry-goods store.

"Yuri, what are you doing?"

"I'm concealing you. Maybe we did get carried away on the dance floor, and I can understand your need to present a certain image in front of the others, but we're alone now." His arms circled her waist and tightened. "Why put off the inevitable? Stay with me tonight."

"No, I—" The words died in her throat as his mouth covered hers and his tongue swept over hers. He lifted her off her feet. Banner gripped his shoulders and kissed him back, but a part of her retreated from the fury of him. She felt as if she were in the eye of a storm and she didn't like the chaos.

"Yuri, please." She made him set her back on her feet, then bent backward over his arms when he tried to kiss her again. "I don't want to be swept off my feet," she said, pushing against his chest. "I want to come to you with slow, sure steps—positive of what I want and why I want it. Can't you understand that?"

He stared at her for a few moments, then sighed. "You have me at a disadvantage."

"How?"

"You're making sense and I'm not," he replied with a half smile before he released her. "What do you expect when you look like that?" he asked, propping his hands at his waist. "The first time I saw you I decided that you were too beautiful for your own good."

"Go on," she scoffed, taking his hand and making him follow her from the inky shadows.

"No, it's true. You look so much like Diana."

Banner glanced up at the cloudy sky in an abject appeal. "There's that name again. Who would have thought that I'd be competing with my mother for a man's attention?"

"No, it's not... That's not what I meant."

"Let's drop it," she suggested, resenting her mother, but for a different reason than before. It was probably silly for her to think that Yuri might be more infatuated with Diana than he was with her, but the feeling persisted. Whatever had been in that diary had been potent enough to drive Yuri from his dedication to his work to a dude ranch in Oklahoma.

They walked the rest of the way in silence, then stood looking at each other for long, lingering moments when they'd reached the house. Banner wanted to believe that the desire in Yuri's eyes was all because of her, but she couldn't make herself believe it.

"I guess I should..."

Banner nodded. "Yes, I guess you should."

"Will you go on the trail ride tomorrow?"

"Yes."

"Then so will I." He took her hands within his and turned them over to examine the lines across her palms. "Such small hands," he murmured. "But with great strength." He pressed a kiss in each, then curled her fingers around the kisses for safekeeping. "I wish you'd read one particular passage in my father's diary about—"

"No!" Banner reacted blindly, tearing her hands from his and moving away from him. "Will you quit forcing them on me? Can't we be with each other without dragging them into it?"

"Don't you want to know the truth?"

"Don't lecture me on the truth, Yuri," she warned. "I'm not the one who withholds it."

He dipped his head in defeat. "Are we back to that? Are we going to take one step forward only to have you drag us back to the starting place over and over again?"

She went up the steps and stood in a square of light streaming through the front door. Looking at him, she moved sideways until his face was illuminated. His expression was expectant, hopeful.

"All right. I'll forgive you for that particular lie. Let's forget it."

"Thank you." He nodded once in deference. "And I'll forgive you for making such a big deal about my white lie while you wallow in your black ones."

She would have imparted a snappy, singeing comeback, but he melted into the night before she could assemble one.

She squeezed her eyes shut, weathering the storm of her anger, then whirled and thundered through the lobby to her quarters.

Seven

Groans and gasps filled the air as the Rocking Horse guests arrived at Fort Gibson and dismounted. Hands rubbed backsides and eyes rolled heavenward in abject appeals for mercy.

Banner caught Pete's eye and laughed. It was always this way. Everyone wanted to go on longer trail rides, but then they wished for shorter ones after riding to Fort Gibson. Most of the trips at Rocking Horse were paced with the novice in mind, taking no more than four hours on horseback, coming and going. The ride to and from Fort Gibson took eight hours. Three hours were spent at lunch and exploring the old fort and town. Once the guests rolled out of bed at six, rode four hours, consumed lunch, checked out the fort, and rode another four hours back to the ranch, it was nightfall. No activities were planned after dinner, since experience had taught the staff that the guests would be exhausted and in bed by ten, if not earlier.

"What are y'all complaining about?" Pete jested. "Aren't you having fun? Y'all have been looking forward to this trip ever since you got to the ranch!"

"Oh, my aching back," Flo Ferguson moaned as she looped her reins around the hitching post.

"That's not what's aching, dear," her husband said, gingerly rubbing his hips, then moving stiffly to help his daughter from the saddle. "Tired, honey?"

"No! Let's look at the fort!" Fawn skipped ahead, leaving her parents to lag behind.

Banner tied Honey with the other horses. From the corner of her eye she watched Yuri dismount—gingerly, cautiously—then loop his reins over the post. He loosened the saddle, stroked the mount's flank and spoke soothingly in its ear. Banner nodded approvingly. He was kind to animals and children, she thought. Good qualities.

The Russian looked like an American cowboy today, she thought, glancing over his faded jeans, navy-blue shirt, jean jacket and scuffed boots. He moved away from his horse, but stopped when he caught sight of her. She smiled, tucked her fingers in the back pockets of her jeans and walked slowly toward him.

"How are you feeling after four hours in the saddle?" she asked.

He removed his black hat and ran his fingers through his hair, mussing it, then smoothing it back into place. "I've come to the conclusion that the greatest invention in the history of mankind is the automobile. I think we should erect a shrine for Henry Ford."

She laughed with him, then poked a finger in his side. "I thought you were in shape. I guess you've been sitting behind a desk for too many months."

One of the horses fidgeted and stamped its hooves in the dirt, drawing Banner's attention. She went to it and loosened the saddle's belly strap. The horse calmed down immediately. "There you go, fella. Did your tenderfoot forget to take care of you?"

"It figures," Yuri said, dryly. "They're all too concerned with their own aches and pains to worry about their horses. So this is Fort Gibson." Yuri stood back to take in the fortress walls constructed of massive logs. "Impressive."

"I thought you'd be interested in it," Banner said, standing beside him. "When you told me about your work on space stations and likened them to outposts and forts, I thought then that you'd enjoy this trip." She fell into step with him as he started for the entrance. "This was a bad-luck fort."

"Oh? Because of Indian raids?"

"No, because of disease. It was rampant here. When a soldier received orders to come here he wrote out his will. It was common knowledge then that a soldier at this fort wouldn't be felled by an arrow, but by disease. There's a graveyard down the street that's full of soldiers who died of consumption, malaria and other types of fevers carried by insects."

"In other words, this place was a death sentence."

"Right."

They walked into the courtyard where a cannon and stocks were the centerpieces. Visitors were taking turns sticking their hands and heads into the stocks and getting their pictures taken in the confinement.

"Want to get in line?" Banner asked, angling an amused glance at Yuri as he watched the others wait impatiently for their turn in the stocks.

"No, thanks. Imprisonment of any kind holds no interest for me."

"Ooo, you're so serious!" She tucked one hand in the crook of his arm and pulled him away from the activity.

"We can't have that. Cheer up, Yuri. You're on vacation, remember?"

He stopped to peek inside a narrow, dirt-floored room and a frown pinched his face.

"Spacious, isn't it?" Banner asked, leaning over the threshold and being engulfed by a dusky odor. "And this was one of the *officer's* quarters! Look, there's an old trunk." She let go of his arm and went inside to the rusty trunk, and opened it. Its interior was tattered and dirty. "Wonder how old this is." Banner turned back to find that Yuri was still outside. He walked on, out of view, and she left the room and caught up with him. "Are you trying to ditch me?"

"No, I'm just not interested in exploring dismal, dank rooms. What's up there?" he asked, pointing to a tower.

"That's the lookout. Want to go up?"

"Yes. You go up first and I'll follow."

He steadied her as she started up the ladder, his hands riding lightly at her waist. When Banner reached the top, she went to the far wall, where holes had been bored through the wood. Turning around, she watched as Yuri surfaced. Pinpoints of light streamed through the holes and lanced across him. One slanted across his eyes, giving them an unearthly glow.

"What's that all about?" he asked, indicating the wall behind her.

"They stuck the barrels of their rifles through these holes and shot the enemy. The higher ones are eyeholes so they could see what they were shooting." She turned back around and peered through at the rolling landscape. "Come and look. The view is gorgeous."

He stood beside her and gazed out at the verdant hills, thickly crowned by trees and shrubs.

"It must have looked similar to this back then," he mused aloud. "Omit the highway, telephone poles and roofs and you can almost imagine what the soldiers saw a century ago."

"Indian territory," Banner said, letting her imagination block out the signs of civilization. "This land is marked by tragedy, treachery and greed."

"Ah, well," Yuri said with a sigh as he stepped back from the view. "Every country has its warts, its periods in history when the fabric of mankind was flawed."

"Where did you live in Moscow?" Banner asked, sensing his reflective mood. "An apartment house?"

"Yes." He pressed his back against the wall and slid down on his haunches. "A small apartment in a big building. We knew all our neighbors. It was like having an extended family." He looked up at her and smiled at the way the light had created a halo around her head. "Two bedrooms. I slept with my brothers and my sister slept with my mother."

"Not much privacy," Banner said, sitting cross-legged near him.

"No, but that's Moscow. It's teeming with humanity."

"And is it true that there are lines upon lines of people?"

"Yes." He nodded, amused by her eagerness for knowledge. He saw it as a good sign. She was giving in to her curiosity. "You've heard of those, have you?"

"I read somewhere that you have to stand in line to get things like tissues and sugar. Is everything difficult to get there?"

"Not everything, but there is rationing. You can't go into one store and buy everything on your shopping list as you do here. Shops are specialized in Russia, so there are lines for bread, meat and staples like sugar and flour. The lines teach Russians the fine art of patience. All good things come to those who wait." He grinned. "That's a saying Americans share with Soviets, except that here you wait in line for concert tickets and films instead of food and toiletries."

"What did you think of America when you first arrived?" Banner asked, fascinated with this glimpse of him. It was as if there were two Yuri Zaarbos. One Russian and one American. One foreign and one familiar.

"I thought it was the promised land, and I was a little terrified of all the opulence." He sighed and sat down solidly, looking around at the dancing light and motes of dust that filtered through it. "This reminds me of your tree—dream house."

"Yes, you're right," she said, giving a cursory glimpse to her surroundings. "But you were telling me about your impressions of America," she reminded him, wanting more insight to the Yuri she didn't know well. She admired him for embarking on such an adventure. She would have been terrified to make such a drastic change in her life, but Yuri had survived and she wanted to know how he'd managed it.

"Well, I wasn't dumbstruck," he assured her. "I was...cautious of all that was suddenly at my disposal. Cars, homes, clothes, restaurants, shopping malls." He shook his head and his eyes widened with remembered shock. "It boggled my mind at first. I'd come here for freedom, and it occurred to me that I might overdose on it."

Banner laughed at the notion, then realized he was serious.

"I decided that I should proceed carefully. I bought a used car, leased a modest apartment and saved my money until I had enough for a down payment on my condo. I bought a few clothes and the essentials of American life. A color TV and stereo, a microwave oven and a VCR," he said, listing them on his fingers.

Banner giggled, delighted by his gentle ridicule of good old American materialism. "You're right. Those things might have replaced Mom, baseball and apple pie."

"The VCR introduced me to American life more than anything else. Through your vast array of films, I learned about America's history, people and passions. A few months after I arrived, however, I found a magical place."

She sat forward, intrigued by the light of passion that had sprung into his eyes. "What? Where?"

"The library." He said it as if it were sacred. "A *public* library! I remember the first time I stepped inside...." His eyes grew misty as he lifted his gaze upward in search of that precious memory. "I almost cried when I saw all those books! Thousands and thousands of them! And all I had to do was to choose one." He sighed expansively. "The only problem was that I wanted them all."

"Aren't there libraries in Russia?"

"Books are as precious as gold in Russia. More precious," he amended solemnly. "Remember when you asked what I did on weekends, and you laughed when I said I read?"

"Yes." Banner nodded, suddenly feeling ashamed of her reaction now that she realized how deeply Yuri cared for literature.

"Well, you couldn't understand what a joy that is for me. To read whatever I wish...that is a luxury. You take it for granted, but it is a privilege that I'll never take lightly. I have spent more money on books than on anything else. My home is filled with them."

"Can I tell you something?" she asked, her throat tightening with an emotion she couldn't name. "I admire you."

He jolted backward with surprise. "Admire me? Why?"

"Because you had the courage to completely change your life." She shook her head, unable to express her thoughts adequately. "That takes a special kind of courage. I don't think I could have done what you did. Weren't you lonely? Weren't you afraid?"

"Yes, but I had a mission."

"What?"

"To succeed. Success will make it all worthwhile. I'll fail only if I don't live up to my potential. My father wrote that same thing in his diary. He was successful here. More successful than he could ever have been in Russia. No matter what pain he endured or inflicted, he made it all worthwhile because he contributed to this society."

"You worry about that, don't you?" she asked, picking up on the desperation in his voice. "That's what drives you."

"If I don't achieve more here than I could in Russia, then my decision to come here was wrong," he explained. "I would have left my family and friends for nothing."

"So you still feel a responsibility to them," she noted with a wry note. "You're still carrying the burden of a responsibility that was given, not taken. Did you come here for them or for you?"

He stared at her blankly for a few moments, then he grinned when he recognized his own words. "I believe that Shakespeare would have said that I've been hoisted with my own petard," he said, laughing under his breath.

"Shakespeare!" Banner said, amazed by the way he quoted literature and poetry with an expert's ease. "How did you learn so much when you've only been here a couple of years?"

"Shakespeare is universal, Banner Bright." He reached for one of her hands and sandwiched it between his own. "We read him even in Russia. However, it's been said that I have a mind like a steel trap. My supervisor at NASA believes that I have a photographic memory."

"Do you?"

He shrugged. "Perhaps. I've never put it to the test." His thoughts brought a scowl to his face. "Your government was pleased by my recall. They kept me in a 'safe house' for two months and interviewed me endlessly."

"Did you give away Soviet secrets?"

His glance was sharp and guarded. "That's classified, Banner."

"Oh, sorry."

He let go of her hand and stood up. "Suffice it to say that if I ever find myself on Soviet soil I'll be a dead man."

She looked up at him, cold with the knowledge that he had endured more than he could tell. Voices drifted to them as a few of the others made their way up the ladder.

"We're being invaded," Yuri said, helping her to her feet. "Privacy is difficult to find even in America."

They left the lookout tower and strolled across the green courtyard to explore the cannon. Frank Ferguson insisted on taking their picture while they posed near the cannon, then gave the Polaroid shot to Banner. She tucked it in her shirt pocket as she tucked away memories of Yuri in the corner of her mind. On second thought, she took the photo from her pocket and pressed it into Yuri's hand.

"No, you keep it," he said.

"No." She closed his fingers around the photograph. "'And when you're old and nodding by the fire, take down this book and slowly read.' Someone once said something like that, but I don't remember who," she confessed.

"It doesn't matter." He slipped the photo into the inner pocket of his jacket. "I'll remember you for saying it."

They took their bag lunches, packed by Cookie, outside the fort and away from the others. Finding a bright patch of sun on the west side of the stockade, they sat down to munch on crispy fried chicken, sweet pickles, tart apples and homemade biscuits. Yuri went to a nearby filling station to buy them cans of soda and candy bars.

They watched the small-town life unfold around them. A postman stopped to chat before continuing his rounds at a leisurely pace. Two stray dogs visited and accepted food scraps. A carload of teenagers hooted and giggled at the grumpy filling-station attendant when he scolded them for "making enough noise to wake the dead." A new mother pushed a carriage and hummed a lullaby as she passed Banner and Yuri. A truck driver returned from a long trip and was met in his front yard by his anxious wife.

"Oh, darling," his wife said, her voice floating across the street to Yuri and Banner. "I was getting worried about you."

"I'm home now, sweetheart," the strapping trucker reassured her, folding the small woman in a warm embrace. "I missed you, babe."

"I made a pot of beans and it'll just take me a minute to bake some cornbread. Oh, I'm so glad you're home."

They kissed, then went into their modest home.

"Someone to come home to," Yuri said, staring across the street at the whitewashed bungalow. "That's the thing I miss most." His gaze swung to Banner's tender expression and he smiled sadly. "I was raised in a house filled with noise. Silence is unnatural in a home."

"What's your mother like? I guess she's strong. A real matriarch."

He wiped his mouth, then his fingers on a napkin. His brows met in a thoughtful scowl, and it was long moments before he answered. "We were awed by her courage and self-preservation. I saw her as a long-suffering, brave woman."

"She is, isn't she?"

"Not really." He reclined on his side, propping himself up on one elbow. "She led us to believe that our father left without so much as a 'so long and good luck,' but that wasn't the case. In my father's diary he wrote of his plans to defect and how he discussed them with his wife. It was not a sudden thing, as I'd been led to believe. He told my mother he would send for the family when he was settled, that he would do everything in his power to reunite us, but my mother refused to leave Russia."

"Were there problems in their marriage?" Banner asked, studying his face intently for every nuance of expression.

"No, not really. It was a case of a simple woman being married to a man of great ambition. My mother understood my father's dilemma, but she didn't see any reason to uproot herself because of it. She encouraged him to go because she knew he would die artistically if he didn't, but she didn't want to go with him. Leaving Russia was crucial to his sanity, but not to hers."

"You mean, she never told you that your father wanted his family with him in America?"

"That's right. She kept it to herself."

"Why?"

"Good question." One side of his mouth tilted up in a half smile. "I can only surmise that it made my mother seem more tragic and created sympathy for her. She was an innocent in my father's treason that way, you see? It was less trouble for her."

"But didn't it cause resentment among your brothers and sister? Didn't they—you—feel deserted...abandoned?"

"Oh, yes. Very much so." He shrugged. "It disturbed me when I read my father's account of what happened, but I was glad to have his side of the story." His gaze was direct and probing. "There are two sides to every story, every situation. Knowing both gave my life balance. Balance leads to peace of mind."

Banner turned her face aside. Back to Diana and Vladimir, she thought. Every discussion ended with them. Yuri's constant references were eroding her defenses and opening her mind to new twists and turns.

"Is that what you wanted me to read in his diary?" she asked, surrendering momentarily to his persistence.

"No. I wanted you to read a passage that concerns your mother and how she grieved for you. It's very touching."

Banner's gaze swung slowly back to his. "What does it say?"

He flung back his head and closed his eyes as he searched for the words. "Let me think... you should read it. I can't recall the exact wording."

"Try. Paraphrase. I'd like to hear this."

Her caustic tone didn't go unnoticed. Yuri opened his eyes and leveled her sarcasm with a piercing glare. Only when she lowered her lashes in submission did he speak again.

"'My poor Diana. A little light has gone from her eyes,'" he said, his voice a raspy whisper as he quoted from his father's diary. "'When she sees a child, she turns away. When she sees a young girl, she weeps openly. I know the pain she suffers, for I suffer the same pain, but I can't alleviate her sense of loss. Diana and I are guilty of loving too much and too late.'"

Banner wanted to turn away, but she couldn't. Her eyes burned, and then Yuri's face undulated as tears brimmed in her eyes before slipping down her cheeks. She swallowed with difficulty and tried to ward off the shame that was welling up inside of her.

"I think we can rest assured that you do have a photographic memory," she said, trying to smile. "You quoted that exactly, didn't you?"

"I believe so." He reached out and his thumb smoothed across her cheek, wiping away her tears. "She loved you, Banner. Why is that so hard to accept? She left you in good hands, in the hands of a man she trusted and admired. Custody battles are destructive, and she didn't want to put you through one. She didn't want to inflict the hectic lifestyle of an artist on an innocent child, even for short periods of time. She wanted you to be raised in a home full of love and security, not bounced back and forth like a tennis ball."

"But why did she leave me in the first place? She could have painted her pictures at the ranch!"

"Would you have been happier if she'd stayed? Would you have enjoyed watching her tolerate your father and resent the life he gave her? Luke and Diana were mismatched. My mother and my father were mismatched. But when Diana met Vladimir it was as if two halves had become whole. What's so terrible about that?" He sat up and held her hands in his. "Diana had a talent, not for riding horses or being hostess at a dude ranch, but for art. She went to New York and studied. Then she visited Paris, Rome, Brussels and London until galleries began to take notice of her work. And she was magnificent, Banner!" His voice lifted with admiration. "Haven't you taken time to view her work? It's beautiful! What a waste to the world if she had stayed at the ranch and only dabbled in greatness."

"My father was like an empty shell after she left," Banner said, watching Yuri's thumbs move back and forth across the back of her hands. "You can't know how...I hated to watch him pining for her."

"Of course you did, but would you have rather watched him live with a woman who didn't love him?"

"No, I guess not," she said with uncertainty.

"Can't you understand how difficult it must have been for your mother to leave?"

She nodded, speechless for a few moments as her mother's feelings mirrored her own. "I'm...like her." It felt as if she'd torn the words from her soul, and she gasped. She'd lost something irretrievable—the bitterness she'd held onto for years. "I want things that I can't find at the ranch," she said, and the admission lifted a weight from her heart.

"What things?"

"I'm not sure, but I know I have to leave to find them. After Dad died I felt so...so unsettled. I feel guilty for wanting to leave."

"Don't," Yuri said, squeezing her hands. "Feel guilty for staying when you don't want to. Feel guilty for those things that you deny yourself for no good reason. Remember, Banner, it's those things we didn't do that we will regret when our lives are at an end."

"Yes, you're right." She looked at him, her eyes bright with tears, and felt a gratitude so great that her heart swelled painfully with it.

Wordlessly, Yuri opened his arms to her and held her close while she cried for the mother's love she had denied and the time she had wasted on things she couldn't change.

"Want to take a shortcut?" Banner asked, reining her horse alongside Yuri's.

"Gladly." He looked ahead at the others. "What about them?"

"I told Pete back at the fort that you and I might take a different route. There's no trail this way, just open country."

"Fine with me."

She smiled and pointed to the east. "It's this way, through these trees, so watch your head."

Bending lower, Banner guided Honey off the trail and along a zigzagging route through the trees. She checked over her shoulder occasionally to make sure that Yuri was close behind. He was leaning over his mount's neck, but handling the horse with skill. The thickly wooded area gave way to a meadow of knee-high prairie grass, and Banner slowed Honey to a walk so that Yuri could catch up.

"Pete says you ride as if you were born to the saddle, and I agree," she said when he'd cleared the woods.

"It's easy when you have a good horse like this one." He stroked the animal's mane, then looked around at the meadow and low hills that banked it. "You know this land like the back of your hand, don't you?"

"Every inch of it," Banner agreed, urging Honey forward. "Yuri, I wanted to thank you for—"

"You don't have to," he interrupted, heading off her expression of gratitude.

"I don't know what got into me at lunch," she said, shyly. "It was kind of you to let me cry on your shoulder."

"I was glad to be there when you needed me."

"I guess it wouldn't hurt me to read your father's diary." She glanced at him through her lashes and smiled when he directed a startled look in her direction. "It's sort of an invasion of privacy, though, don't you think?"

"No. I think my father would have wanted us to read it." He shifted to a more comfortable seat in the saddle and gripped the horn. "I saw a showing of your mother's work in Dallas last year."

Banner pretended to study the low hills, unable to face him with what she had to say. "You're a lot like your father, aren't you? You even fell in love with the same woman." She heard anger in his silence before his voice validated it.

"Banner, I'm not a boy who falls in love with an image in a magazine or in the movies. I admit I was intrigued by Diana, maybe even a little infatuated, but that's as far as my feelings for her go. One doesn't have to love the artist to appreciate her paintings."

She kept her gaze averted so that he couldn't read the doubt in her eyes. "But you came here to meet her daughter and...," she said, leaving the statement open-ended for him to finish.

"And I met her," Yuri said, edging his horse ahead of hers so that he could see her carefully composed expression of disinterest. "So what shadings are you putting on that? Do you actually believe that I came here to make love to her daughter because I couldn't make love to her?"

"What do you think?" she challenged.

"I think you're on the verge of insulting me, that's what I think." He dug his heels into the horse's side, sending it ahead at a gallop.

Honey's ears pricked forward, and she needed no urging from Banner to follow suit. The palomino caught up with Yuri's chestnut gelding and passed it, gaining speed as it raced across the open meadow toward a swell of land. Banner reined to the right and squeezed her knees into Honey's side when Honey started up an incline. She pulled the horse to a stop at the crest and swung from the saddle.

"Why are we stopping?" Yuri asked, pulling sharply on the reins to settle the gelding.

"I want to check on something while we're here." Banner let the reins dangle so that Honey could munch on tender grass while she went toward a thickness of brush along the side of the hill. Pushing aside the thorny branches, she stood back so that Yuri could see the boards slanting across a gaping hole. Two of the boards had fallen away, giving a glimpse of darkness beyond.

"This is the cave I told you about. I used to love this place." She bent double and stepped over the lower boards until she was half in and half out of the cave opening. "Looks like someone tore off those boards to get in here. Probably some deer hunters. We've posted No Trespassing signs, but it's hard to keep them off the land during deer season."

"Are you going in there?" Yuri asked, swinging down from the saddle.

"Yes. Come on."

"No."

"It's neat inside here," she said, motioning for him to follow her. "The walls are damp and there's usually some bats inside. They won't hurt you. It's just a silly, old wives' tale about bats being dangerous. They're harmless."

"No, I don't want to go inside."

The panicky thread in his voice triggered her sixth sense, and she looked at him fully, only then seeing the vestiges of terror in his pitchy eyes and in the pallor of his skin.

"Yuri, are you all right?" she asked, inching out from between the boards and back into the daylight.

"I...yes." He swallowed hard and his hands clenched and unclenched at his sides. "I just don't want to go in there, that's all."

"Okay, if you're sure that's all." She looked back at the barricade. "I just thought it might be fun."

"No, it wouldn't be fun for me."

Banner propped the loose boards into place as she mulled over Yuri's loathing of caves...of dark places. The old cabin, the officer's quarters at the fort, the cave. When she turned back to him, she had a clearer sense of what he was about.

"Are you afraid of the dark?" she asked, moving closer as she spoke and reaching out to grasp his hand, a hand that was too cold for a warm day.

"Afraid of..." He bent his head and released a shaky sigh. "Yes, I suppose I am." He laughed, but there was no sound of amusement in it. "You're looking at a grown man who can't sleep without having a light on. Silly, isn't it?" He tugged his hand from hers and turned away when embarrassment colored his face. "I didn't used to be...I didn't used to have a sense of claustrophobia. It's a holdover from my great escape. I guess you could say that it's part of the dues I paid for passage here."

"Being cargo wasn't fun, I take it."

"No, it wasn't." He smiled at her, but avoided her eyes. "It was...worse than anyone could imagine. I was crated up with only my fear and worries to keep me company. After thirty-two hours, I was on the verge of insanity."

"Thirty-two hours?" Banner repeated, horrified. "You stayed in the crate that long?"

"Yes. It was a long, arduous journey. Dark and damp. I could hear the scurry of rats most of the time." He shuddered and ran his hands up and down his arms. "I suppose I'll get past this in time, but for now I avoid tight places or darkness."

"It's strange," Banner said thoughtfully. "I associate you with dark things. Dark eyes, dark hair. You even wear dark colors." She stood in front of him and stilled his restless hands with hers. "When you told me your last name and I came by your cabin later, thinking you were still awake because the light was on in your bedroom..."

"Yes," he said, smiling at himself. "Like a child afraid of night monsters." He frowned and held her hands against his chest. "I haven't told anyone else about this."

"Your secret is safe with me. In fact, I'll give you a secret of mine to keep."

"What?"

"I'm afraid of change."

"What do you mean?"

She opened up his arms and nestled closer to him, sighing when his arms enfolded her like steel petals. "I just realized it for myself today. I avoid changes. It's silly because everything has to change, doesn't it? The seasons, fashions, places, people. Everything. But it scares me."

"Changes don't have to be bad or traumatic," Yuri said, his voice vibrating in his chest. Banner pressed her ear closer, feeling secure in his arms. "Changes can be good."

"Yes, and so can the dark." She lifted her head and smiled up into his face.

He laughed and kissed her lightly on the lips. "When you're right, you're right. I bet I wouldn't be afraid of it if you were with me."

His implication sent her from his arms. She looked around distractedly, then whistled for Honey.

"We should be going. It will be dusk soon," she said.

She was glad when Yuri didn't comment on her abrupt dismissal. He simply mounted his horse and waited for her to settle herself in her own saddle.

Banner looked across at him, sensing that he was waiting for something else. His eyes held a hundred questions, none of which she was prepared to answer.

"Will you keep my secret?" she asked.

"Yes, but I don't think I'll have to for long. I think you're ready to banish that particular fear from your life."

"You might be right." She looked in the direction they would take, but didn't signal her horse to move. "I have to take one step at a time, Yuri. I'm not the type to run headlong into things." She paused, gathering her courage, then looked directly at him. "Spending the night with you will make a difference in my life."

"In mine, too."

She smiled, touched by his admission and wanting desperately to believe him. For a moment, she was tempted to agree to the proposition in his eyes, in the way he smiled at her.

"I won't press," he said before she could make herself speak. "We're not at odds on this, Banner. I, too, want you to come to me with slow, sure steps." He urged his horse into a walk, then glanced back at her. "But I'll be leaving at the end of the week. We have a lot going for us, but time isn't one of them."

She stared at his straight back and counted the days. Tomorrow was Saturday and Yuri would leave Sunday with the others. She placed a hand to her stomach where her heart seemed to have sunk. When he was right, he was right, she thought. Time had suddenly become her adversary.

Eight

Looking up from the papers on her desk, Banner motioned for Pete to come inside her office.

"DiDi said you wanted to see me before dinner," Pete said, sweeping off his cowboy hat and hanging it on the tree by the door. "What's up?"

"Sit down, Pete." Banner waited for him to lower his lanky frame into the chair across from her desk. "Well, the first guests of the season will leave tomorrow. They seem to have had a good time."

"Oh, sure." Pete nodded eagerly, his blue eyes crinkling at the corners. Deeply tanned, his skin looked leathery and tough from too many hours in the sun. "They had a fine time. The next group will, too, I reckon. Hope the weather's better for the next group. It's been a wet spring so far."

Banner nodded absently, her attention directed more at Pete than at what he was saying. He'd always been a hard worker. Luke had trusted him completely, and so did Banner. Pete took pride in the ranch as if it were his own land. And soon he'll marry DiDi, Banner thought with a quirky smile of sentimentality. Pete and DiDi, two of her favorite people, husband and wife. It had a fitting ring to it.

"Something wrong, Banner?" Pete asked, getting anxious under her appraisal. "Did one of the guests complain about something?"

"No, nothing like that. Pete, you are going to marry DiDi come July, aren't you? You're not just fooling around this time, right?"

"Right." He looked puzzled and shook his head. "Some problem with that?"

"No." She glanced at the literature on her desk and grinned. "Guess what I've been doing today?"

Pete's gaze swept over the desk. "Looks like you've been reading or bookkeeping."

"Not exactly." Banner picked up one of the slim volumes and waved it. "College handbooks, Pete. I've been sitting here looking through them because I've got an inkling to go to college and learn a new trade. What do you think about that?"

"Why, I think . . ." Pete's blue eyes widened and he ran a hand down his face. "I don't know what to think. What started all this? I didn't know you were interested in changing jobs. Will you close the ranch? Sell it, maybe?"

Banner leaped up from the chair and rounded the desk, alarmed by Pete's hasty assumption. "No! I'd never sell the ranch!" She placed both her hands on his muscled forearm and leaned into his face, stressing her seriousness. "I wanted to talk to you about running the place if I do decide to leave for college, but I'm not thinking of closing the ranch down. Pete, do you think I'd throw you out into the cold, just like that?" She shook his arms as if trying to shake some sense into him. "You're my best buddy and you're marrying my best friend, for heaven's sakes!"

Pete nodded and put his callused hand over both of hers. "Right. I wasn't thinking, I guess. I know you've been unsettled of late."

"Yes, and I finally figured out why." Banner dropped to her haunches beside the chair and looked up into Pete's trustworthy face. "I've been trying to be just like Luke, when I'm really more like Diana." Banner searched his expression for any sign of displeasure or disappointment. "Doesn't that kind of shock you?"

Pete chuckled and ran one hand over her silky hair. "Hon, I think you're a little like both of them, but mostly you're just you." He leaned forward and his lips touched her smooth forehead. "If you want to go off to college and learn about things other than horses and ranching, then I'd bet it was because you had a yen for something different, not because of some kind of gene pool."

"Did Dad ever talk to you about Diana?" Banner asked, amazing herself with the question. She'd known Pete for years and had never broached this subject before today.

"Not much. He sure carried a torch for that woman, didn't he? I don't think he ever paid one bit of attention to any other female—besides you, of course."

"She was charismatic," Banner said, using a phrase she'd read in Vladimir's diary, which Yuri had given her after the trail ride. She'd sat up until almost midnight reading the descriptive passages and had awakened with a sense of wellbeing that she hadn't felt since her father's death.

"Charismatic," Pete echoed. "I hear she was a looker, too. Like you."

Banner stood up and ruffled Pete's unruly blond hair. "Sweet-talker," she accused, laughing. "Well, what do you say, cowboy? Will you keep this place running like a well-oiled pocket watch if I take a notion to check out some greener pastures?"

"Why, sure, sugar." Pete winked and gave her a warm smile. "You know you didn't even have to ask."

"It'll mean a salary increase for both you and DiDi."

"Hey, now." Pete shook his head and a worried frown creased his face. "There's no call for that."

"Don't argue with me on this, Pete Parker," Banner warned with good-natured gruffness. "This is business, not personal. I wouldn't think of leaving this place in your hands without increasing your salary. It's only fair." She glanced over the booklets and sat in the desk chair again. "This will always be my home, Pete, but it's just not enough for me anymore. Ever since Dad died, I've been..."

"As restless as the wind," Pete said, grinning. "I couldn't help but notice." He studied his hands minutely and peeked at her through his stubby lashes. "DiDi told me about Yuri being Zaarbo's son. I guess that was the stick of dynamite you needed."

Banner smiled at his description. Yes, Yuri Zaarbo was one explosive personality, she thought.

"Hope you're not mad at DiDi for telling me."

She waved one hand in a dismissive gesture. "No, it's okay. Yuri's the one who let the cat out of the bag."

"Which college are you thinking about?" Pete asked, sitting forward on the edge of the chair to study the booklets.

"I haven't decided." She touched one from a college in Houston, then folded her hands on top of the desk. "There's no hurry. I probably won't apply for admission until summer. I thought I'd take a couple of summer classes to see if I like it before I become a full-time student."

"What are you going to study?"

"Business," she said, then shrugged. "At least until I get a better idea of what I want to do. I still have some choices to make. Speaking of choices, which band did you finally hire for the Happy Trails party tonight?"

"My Uncle Jeb's band." Pete pushed himself up from the chair. "As a matter of fact, I've got to get over to the Shortbranch and see how things are going. They're supposed to be decorating the place for the party." He went toward the door and plucked his hat off the tree. "Has DiDi asked you about being our maid of honor at the wedding?"

"No, not yet."

"That gal sure procrastinates." He grinned and glanced shyly at Banner. "Will you? Do you think you can get away from college and all?"

"I wouldn't miss your wedding for the world," Banner assured him. "I'll be there with bells on."

"Good."

"Who's your best man?"

Pete grinned from ear to ear as he fit his battered hat on his head. "Cookie. It took some fancy talking, but I finally convinced him to stand up for me."

Banner shook her head in amusement. "It should be some kind of wedding, Pete." She waved him off. "See you later. Let me know if there's any problem with the party."

"Okay. I'll catch up with you later."

After Pete had left, Banner simmered comfortably in her newfound peace of mind. She stood up, stretched lazily, and wandered into the living room off the office area. The painting over the fireplace drew her like a magnet. Charisma, she thought as she stopped and appreciated the flow of colors and attention to detail. Reaching up, she touched the signature in the corner, her fingertips running lightly over the graceful lines and curves of it.

"Diana Dufrayne O'Bryan," she murmured, feeling a strong connection to that name for the first time since she was ten. Closing her eyes, she could see her mother's oval-shaped face, ebony hair, wide blue eyes and petallike lips.

Diana's voice drifted to her from some far-off memory, sweet and lilting: Banner Bright, Banner Bright, I love you with all my might. You're the best of him, the best of me. What a fine, lovely lady you'll someday be.

A teardrop rolled down Banner's cheek as the love that rhyme had held came back to her, full-force and heartfelt. She stepped back and wiped the moisture from her eyes, absolving her mother of all her sins, real and imagined.

"I loved you too, Mama," she whispered, using the title of respect she hadn't spoken since she was ten.

A sharp rapping on her office door drew her from her sentimental journey.

"Come in," she called, moving into the office from the living room, and stopping beside her desk when Yuri stepped over the threshold. "Oh, hello." She smiled, wondering if he could read the melancholy in her eyes. "I have something for you." She opened a desk drawer and took the diary from it, then extended it toward him. "It's a real page-turner."

He took the volume from her and tucked it under his arm. "It's not a best-seller."

"It was for me. I was sold on it before I even read the first page." She perched on the edge of her desk, swinging one leg in concession to the tingle of her nerves.

Yuri had broken from his somber colors with a pair of wheat-colored slacks and an olive pullover shirt. He checked the time on his expensive gold watch.

"Late for an appointment?" Banner asked, teasingly.

"No, just counting down the hours."

Her leg stopped swinging and her heart thudded dully in her chest. She closed her eyes for a moment, warding off a sense of doom and desperation. He didn't have to remind her, she thought. She was counting the minutes, the seconds she still had with him.

"Are you going to the party tonight?" she asked, sliding off the desk and pretending to be interested in the papers scattered on her desk.

"The farewell party?" he asked, adding a new shading to her query. "Yes, with you, I hope."

Her heart lifted on fluttering wings. "If you're asking me for a date, I accept." She glanced at him through her lashes. "I don't usually socialize so openly with my guests, but I'll make an exception in your case. I suppose we're all the talk anyway. Flo Ferguson asked me this morning at breakfast if you were my beau."

"Your beau," he repeated, smiling faintly. "What did you say?"

"I said that you were a special friend," she whispered, then watched out of the corner of her eye as he wandered across the office to the bank of windows. He seemed preoccupied, distant.

"After reading that diary do you still believe that your mother left your father for another man?"

"No." She moved to the side of the desk nearest him and leaned back against it. "I judged her too harshly."

"Did the diary give you new insight to her?"

"Somewhat," she admitted, staring at his straight back and wide shoulders. Rays glinted off his dark hair and lined his profile with soft light. She recalled their first turbulent meeting not so long ago, but eons ago in emotional time. "Vladimir's diary gave me a better picture of you more than anything else."

"Of me?" He turned his head, lifting one brow in speculation. "How could it? I wasn't mentioned except in general terms."

Banner laughed softly and crossed one ankle over the other, adopting a more comfortable attitude with him. "You're so much like him, Yuri. The parallels are so clearly drawn." She waited for him to turn slowly, meeting her gaze with eyes that questioned. "Your passion for your work, his passion for his music. Your torturing doubts about whether you did the right thing in coming here, his same torturing doubts. Your homesickness for your family, his homesickness. It's all there."

"Ah, but he was luckier than me. He found a woman who cared for him, who understood him."

Unable to withstand his penetrating eyes, she straightened and looked at her desk, then grabbed one of the booklets.

"I've been looking through these college handbooks," she said, breathlessly, desperately. "I've had them around for a couple of years. I guess, subconsciously, I was interested in college or I wouldn't have sent off for these."

He walked over to her desk and glanced over the handbooks, then picked up the one from Houston, turning it around for her to see its cover.

"Texas isn't on the other side of the world. You could come visit me, if you wanted." He selected a pen from a silver holder and jotted something on the cover of the book. "This is my address. It's easy to find, providing you want to find it." He reached for her hand and placed the booklet in it. "Don't lose that."

"I won't," she promised. When he started for the door, she asked in alarm, "Where are you going?"

"To my cabin." He arched an expressive brow. "Something wrong with that?"

"No, I..." She looked around, trying to find something that would make him stay a while longer. "Would you like some coffee? How about a drink? A beer?"

He smiled, amused by her coffee, tea or soft-drink approach. "No, thanks." He started to turn away, then froze and looked at her in a way that made her temperature soar. "I can see the door closing on the woman I hunger for, and it's difficult for me, Banner." His hand curved around the doorknob. "I want to be with you during these last few hours, but I can't bring myself to make small talk or to act as if you're just a special friend I've made during my vacation."

When she didn't move or make a sound, he gave a sigh of sharp impatience, tossed the diary into the nearest chair and closed the distance between them. His mouth claimed hers, branding her with a hot, fiery intensity. She made a mewling, helpless sound as her arms circled his neck and her body arched into his. His hands moved down her back, under her shirt, then up over her skin in a warm winnowing caress that sifted through her jumbled feelings and found her passion. When his lips left hers, Banner opened her eyes and ran her fingers through his hair with aching familiarity. She pressed a wayward swath into place at his temple, then smoothed the flecks of white amid the ebony strands.

"We'll leave the party early," she said, letting her eyes say the rest.

He smiled and went back to the door, opening it with no hesitance this time. He retrieved the diary, running the flat of his hand over the leather cover as if it held magic or good luck. "I'll come by around eight for you," he said, then touched the corner of the diary to his forehead in a quick salute. "I'm glad you read this. See you later."

The Happy Trails party had never been so wrought with sentiment, Banner thought as she followed Yuri's slow, sure steps in time with the ballad. She leaned her cheek against the front of his black shirt, filled her senses with his distinct aroma of masculinity, and tried to concentrate on the lyrics. They held a special meaning for her. She'd heard the song before—many times before—but she'd never felt each and every word as if the song had been written for her and for this particular hour in time.

I'm not a vision; I'm not a dream; I'm a woman, she chanted mentally with the singer, then looked up into Yuri's eyes. "You're not a hope; you're not a wish; you're a man. Loving each other isn't something we planned, but it's only a matter of time."

"What did you say?" Yuri asked, making Banner suddenly aware that she had spoken the last lines aloud.

"I was just singing along," she said, feeling a wave of color spread over her face, then smiling at an expression she couldn't read on his. "What are you thinking about?"

"How pretty you look tonight," he said, stepping back to admire her tight-waisted, calico-printed dress of blues and greens. "Wonder what you'll look like in a business suit."

"A business suit?" She shook her head, confused.

"After you graduate you'll have to dress for success," he said, trying to look serious, but failing. "No more peasant dresses, jeans, leather jackets and the like."

"You can take the girl out of the country, but not the country out of the girl," she said. "I'll dress as I like, business or no business."

"Good. I like the way you dress." He placed his hands at her waist, spanning it easily. He looked startled when a few of the guests began singing a wobbly version of "Auld Lang Syne." Banner started to join in, but he pressed a finger to her lips. "No, let's not sing that. It's too sad. Too final."

"It's a sweet, sentimental song," she protested.

"It speaks of forgetting old acquaintances and I don't want to forget." His lips replaced his finger. "I want to remember...everything."

He took one of her hands and led her from the dance area, across the polished floor and outside into the warm spring night. Stars lit up the sky and a half-moon hung like a bright sickle among them.

"Yuri, Banner!" Flo Ferguson came forward, followed by her husband. "We wanted to tell you how wonderful it's been being with you the past two weeks. We'll miss this place and you."

"Come back next year," Banner said.

"We hope to," Frank said, then looked past them into the saloon. "Is the party over?"

"No." Yuri moved away from the door to let them enter. "We stepped out for a breath of air."

"So did we." Flo touched his arm and smiled warmly. "I'll think of you every time I watch a shuttle launch."

"It was nice to meet you. If you're ever in Houston, look me up. I'd be glad to give you a tour of NASA."

"Great!" Frank pumped his hand. "We might do that!"

Yuri turned to watch them enter the saloon. "I don't even know where they live," he said.

"Kansas City," Banner told him, linking an arm in his and leading him away from the Shortbranch. "They have an eighteen-year-old son who used to come here with them. Fawn, I gather, was a surprise but a welcome one. Flo told me that she had given up the hope of having another child, but life has its little ironies."

"What's their son's name?"

"Freddy."

Yuri laughed, shaking his head. "Frank, Flo, Freddy and Fawn Ferguson. Fascinating."

"Funny," Banner said, laughing with him.

"Faddish," he added.

"Fashionable," Banner corrected.

"Fatuous," Yuri insisted, frowning, but still laughing.

"Fanciful," she argued.

"Fetching."

"Fetching?"

"You." He smiled. "Feral."

"Feral?"

"My desire for you."

"Forthright."

"That's me," he agreed, then lowered his brows when she tugged him away from the lane that led to the main house. "Where are we going?"

"Your place." She angled a glance at him. "Any objections?"

"Not from me." He sought out her gaze again. "Still don't want a man in your bedroom, huh?"

"Nothing like that," she objected. "I don't want to be disturbed. My quarters are like Grand Central Station at times. People tend to drop by to tell me how much fun they had here, how they hope to come back, how they'd like to make reservations for next year, etcetera, etcetera, etcetera."

"Say no more."

He took her hand and made her run with him to his cabin. They were both out of breath when they arrived, filling the quiet living room with their rasping gasps for air. Banner dropped her purse into a chair and kicked off her heels, feeling strangely at home and blissfully relaxed. Where had her nerves gone? Where was that streak of trepidation she'd struggled against ever since promising him this night, this private showing of her desire for him?

Feeling flushed and expectant, she looked to Yuri for guidance. He tapped a finger to his forehead as if he'd remembered something.

"I have a gift for you."

"A gift?" she echoed, wondering exactly what he meant. He was all the gift she wanted.

"Yes." He went into the bedroom and came back, dangling a gold chain from his fingers. "Something to remember me by." He handed her the necklace. "Go on. Take it. I want you to have it."

She examined the gold letters, Russian letters that held no meaning for her. Looking at him, she shrugged helplessly.

"It's the Russian word for peace," he explained, then took it and stepped behind her to latch it at the back of her neck. "I got it at an antinuclear rally a few years ago."

"An antinuclear rally?" she repeated, laughing incredulously.

"You didn't think we had those in Russia, did you?" he asked, turning her around so that he could see the necklace against her skin. "Well, that kind of news doesn't travel far in Russia, but we do have demonstrations." He lifted his brows and smiled contritely. "Quiet, careful ones." Touching the golden letters with a forefinger, he let his gaze drift up to her face. "Now that you've found peace of mind, I hope you keep it."

"I don't need anything to remember you by," she said, her hand lifting to caress the symbolic letters nestled at the base of her throat. "But I appreciate the thought behind this. Speak some Russian. I want to hear it."

"No." He ran a hand over her head in a gentle way. "To you, I speak only English. I want you to understand every word I say." When she closed her eyes his lips touched one eyelid, then the other. "I want no misunderstandings between us, Banner Bright. No more guessing or white lies or black ones. Only the truth... in a language we both understand." His hands framed her face. "Look at me."

She opened her eyes to the raw passion in his.

"Who do you see?"

She blinked in confusion, then answered, "You. I see Yuri Zaarbo."

"And I see you. Banner O'Bryan." He looked around the room, then back to her. "*They* aren't here. We're alone."

She smiled, catching his meaning. "Diana and Vladimir?"

"Yes. It's just you and I. Their past brought us to this moment, but we're on our own from here on in." He walked past her to the bedroom, turning to face her before he crossed over the threshold. "Will you come to me with slow, sure steps?"

He held out one hand and she went with him, knowing who she wanted and why she wanted him.

Nine

The bedside lamp spilled a golden glow into the room, giving everything soft, fuzzy edges. Banner stood at the foot of the bed, watching as Yuri pulled back the simple spread and cotton sheet with one hand while he unbuttoned his shirt with the other. He tugged on his shirt, pulling it from his waistband until the tails hung in soft wrinkles. Banner felt his amusement before she lifted her gaze to his smile.

"What are you waiting for? An invitation?"

She shrugged, glancing around the room and wondering how to begin, how to set time in motion again. "You're obviously better at this than I am. Experience pays off, I guess."

"Oh, Banner." His tone held many things: impatience, understanding and just the barest hint of anxiety. He walked around the bed to her with light, rhythmic steps that made her think of a wolf's tread. Ropes of muscle flexed across his shoulders and down his chest when he lifted his hands to frame her face. "I've been with others, yes. But this is the first time in my life that I have the right woman for the right reasons at the right time."

She touched his lips with trembling fingertips. "Do you remember that day in the stables when you kissed me?"

"Of course."

"I was so frightened of you!" Her sapphire eyes widened with the memory of what she'd felt. "You were far too tempting, far too bold for a stranger."

"I never felt like a stranger with you. Are you frightened of me now?"

"No, not now." She placed her hands on his chest, and her fingertips nestled into the dark, downy hair. His skin felt warm against her cool hands. "We were never strangers to each other," she said, more for her revelation than for his. "It's as if I knew you existed and I'd meet you eventually." She looked into his eyes with a sense of wonder. "Did you feel that way about me?"

"Absolutely. Didn't I tell you that fate was pulling the strings? We didn't plan this; it was planned for us."

She smiled tremulously and tried to banish the niggling doubt from her mind and heart. When he talked of fate conspiring with them, she worried that he was caught up in a fantasy while she was holding on to reality.

"'I'm not a vision; I'm not a dream; I'm a woman,'" she said, reciting the song she'd identified with earlier. "'You're not a hope; you're not a wish; you're a man.'"

He tipped his head to one side in a show of puzzlement, but his smile was enchanting. "That's right, sweet Banner."

Slowly, seductively, he dropped to his knees before her; his hands riding lightly at her waist, his gaze lifted to hers. His mouth opened, then moved against the fabric covering her stomach. His breath seared through the thin material, warming a patch of her skin.

The unexpected gesture brought tears to her eyes. She rested her hands on the back of his head, her fingers delving through fine, silky strands. His hair was the same color as hers, but it felt entirely different. Hers was thick and weighty, but his felt airy, glossy, baby soft. She bent over and kissed the crown of his head. He cupped her hips, exploring her curves with kneading fingers.

Yuri sat back on his heels, pulled her closer and his hot mouth slipped down to the juncture of her legs. His breath seeped through her skirt, adding more heat to what was already there. Her legs trembled and her knees grew weak in their effort to support her limp body.

Banner slipped her hands under his shirt and gripped his shoulders for support. She was thankful for this prelude, grateful for the time to get used to this man and his way of loving. Her fluttering nerves had settled, overruled by her mounting passion.

"Yuri, Yuri," she whispered, folding her arms like sheltering angel's wings around his head. "Yuri Zaarbo." She laughed lightly. "Suddenly, I love that name. Zaarbo. Zaarbo. Zaarbo!" Never had a name held such enchantment, such allure.

Warm, slightly callused hands moved up under her skirt from her calves to her thighs, whispering against her nylons. He moved his head from side to side, nuzzling the heart of her femininity while his fingers slipped under the waistband of her nylons and peeled them slowly from her slim legs. She used his shoulders to balance herself, raising one foot and then the other until the nylons were gone, tossed to one side ceremoniously. Yuri lifted her skirt, then let it billow over his head.

Banner laughed again and smoothed her hands over the lump under her skirt that was his head. "I thought you were afraid of the dark," she teased.

"Not this kind of dark," he said, his lips moving against her satiny panties.

She unbuttoned her tight cuffs, then freed the buttons on the front of her dress. She slipped the fabric off her shoulders and let it pool at her waist while Yuri's lips slid over her stomach, his tongue leaving a moist trail. She thrilled to the rough slickness that ran across her belly, tickled her waist, explored her navel. Then she stepped back from his titillating tongue and lips, her skirt trailing over his head until his face was revealed to her again.

Her eyes flirted with his as she pushed the dress down and kicked it aside with one foot. She trembled before him, all glowing skin and strips of satin and lace. Her eyes were enormous jewels, glittering with excitement and nervous elation.

He kneeled before her, an ardent worshiper before a shrine of femininity.

She touched the necklace he'd given her, reading the word on it with her fingers and knowing it in her heart.

Yuri got to his feet and unfastened his thin belt and then his trousers, but didn't remove them. He moved closer, his hands slipping over her back and then up into the cascade of her hair. Banner lifted her lips to his, seeking and eager. She closed her eyes to more fully experience his sipping kisses that left her lips trembling for more.

He tipped her head to one side and his mouth slanted across hers, sweet and satisfying. His soft, moist kisses absorbed her so completely she was unaware that he'd unhooked her bra until the straps fell off her shoulders. The bra was discarded, followed by his shirt. Banner wound her arms about his neck and her breasts flattened against hair-roughened skin. His eyes looked like wet onyx to her, shimmering and precious.

"My dark, brooding Russian," she whispered, then wondered if her mother had said the same thing to this man's father. Had Diana trembled like this? she wondered. Did she look into eyes as black as these and see heaven and earth? Did his smile hold her like a Gypsy's spell?

Banner hid her face in the curve of his neck, overcome by life's complexities, then oblivious to them when she was lowered to a plain of cool cotton sheets.

His loving was like a gentle storm, nourishing her barren places and encouraging growth and blooming things within her. When his body settled on top of hers, Banner ran her hands up and down his back and hips. He felt solid but flexible, rough but tender, and so many other contradicting things that she couldn't name them all. His tongue parried with hers, but was the victor in the end, stealing her breath and leaving her limp with desire. He slipped down her body like a cool breeze, dropping kisses upon her breasts and stomach.

After removing the last barrier of lacy satin, he threaded his fingers between hers and imprisoned her hands at her sides. His lips skimmed across her inner thighs, finding pleasure points she hadn't known existed. Did he know her body better than she did? Banner wondered incoherently, her head moving back and forth in wild abandon as she squeezed her eyes shut and let a current of passion take her toward the sea of fulfillment she knew was right around the bend.

His carefully orchestrated seduction gratified her. She should have known that he would be a consummate lover, she thought dazedly; should have known he'd be a pampering lover, a patient lover.

He let go of her hands, and with her eyes closed, Banner waited for the next assault on her senses. The tap of a belt buckle against the floor snapped her from her suspension and her eyes flew open. Her lips parted in a soft gasp as she sat up in the center of the bed. Her pulse quickened as she reached out, her fingertips gliding ever so lightly down his chest, over the ripple of muscle at his waist and into the black forest of crisp hair below his navel.

Why did the poets sing the praises of the female form and the sculptors shape the curves of breasts and nipped waists when a man's body held such glory? she pondered, rising to her knees so that the flat of her hands could span the width of his shoulders.

His thighs were thick with sinew, bulging with muscle. His chest was defined by the thrust of pectorals and the sleek ridges of ribs. Blue-tinted veins ran down his arms and up the column of his throat. Banner kissed the corner of his mouth, nibbling and teasing him. She trembled, but remained perfectly still as Yuri's hands molded her breasts, and he took one bright pink tip between his lips.

"You're beautiful," she murmured, sliding her hands over the tops of his shoulders. "So beautiful!"

"You...are beautiful," he whispered, his lips touching hers with a feathery lightness. "Not me. You."

He lifted her breasts up to the pleasure of his flicking tongue and suckling mouth. Her nipples gathered into pebbles of flesh and an aching, burning need pulsated through her. Banner flung back her head, her hair sweeping across her back, her throat vibrating with moaning sobs of submission. When she could stand it no longer, she fell back across the bed and he followed her.

The lower part of his body fit perfectly between her thighs. His arms bracketed her head. His eyes bored into hers. The tip of his tongue skimmed across her lips and he smiled, warming her heart.

"You give me such pleasure," he murmured, punctuating his words with tender kisses. "I look at you and I can hardly believe that this is happening...that it's not a dream."

His body thrust forward against hers in a rehearsal that left her wanting the real performance. She gripped his hips, guiding him instinctively between her moist, clinging walls. The thrust of his tongue into her mouth sent her over the edge, and she cried out garbled words of joy and tribute.

"I love you, I love you," he chanted between drugging kisses, and his voice sounded broken as if he were close to tears. "I've loved you for such a long time...forever."

She accepted his proclamation with mixed feelings, telling herself that he was spouting lover's poetry, not something to be taken literally because he couldn't have loved *her* for a long time...only days or weeks. Poetry, her mind argued with the other chiding voice in her head. It's nothing but poetry...a lover's lament. He wasn't confusing her with a dream lover.

Gratefully, the driving movement of his body into hers vanquished the punishing thoughts from her mind, and she joined him in a lover's dance that she knew instinctively, intimately. She kissed the hollow of his shoulder and held tightly as a sheen of perspiration coated their bodies, making their flesh slip like a hand into a glove, a comet into infinity.

The lamp's glow illuminated his face, giving her glimpses of the myriad emotions flitting through his eyes, tightening his lips, creasing his brow. She watched the desire build in him, felt it within her, shared it when it burst forth like flashes of lightning. His sigh of repletion pleased her, and she felt the glow of a woman who had been loved completely and skillfully by a man who approached lovemaking as an art connoisseur would approach an early Van Gogh. He hadn't just performed the act of love; he had lived it, worshipping her, respecting her, involving her in every nuance, every particle of feeling.

"Oh, Yuri," she whispered, smoothing his hair back from his forehead. She wanted to say something profound to him, but could think of only simple things—love, appreciation, gratitude. "You're...everything," she said, laughing at her lacking vocabulary.

He shifted against her, throwing shadow, then there was a click and the room was drenched in darkness. Banner looked toward the dark where the lamp had glowed seconds ago.

"Yuri," she whispered, suddenly afraid for him. "The dark..."

His lips caressed hers assuringly, lessening her momentary panic for his well-being.

"Tonight," he said, his voice as cleansing as summer rain, "you will be my light."

Summer blazed over Oklahoma like a prairie fire, blistering the atmosphere and wilting spring's flowers. The bird songs sounded listless, and the drone of bees was sepulchral as if they, too, mourned the passing of spring.

Banner stretched lazily in her tree house and gazed through the leafy branches at a patch of sky. Hearing the approach of horses, she propped herself up on one elbow and cautioned herself to remain quiet and hidden as she watched Pete and twenty-five guests ride closer to her sanctuary. They'd been on a trail ride since early morning, but there was still merriment in their smiles and voices. Pete's voice lifted above the others to draw attention to landmarks, nature's wonders and snippets of cowboy folklore.

He was doing a good job, Banner thought, and the guests loved him. Nothing like a handsome, rugged cowboy to make a dude ranch vacation something to remember. Pete was a man for all seasons, indulging in friendly flirting with the women, man-to-man rap sessions with the men and gentle teasing with the children.

Banner had prepared herself for a fit of depression when she'd turned over the operation of the dude ranch to Pete at the beginning of May, but her spirits had never drooped over the past two weeks. She didn't miss the trail rides, the mixing with the guests, the congenial lunches and dinners. No. In fact, she *loved* sleeping in, lunching with DiDi, dining with Cookie in the big kitchen, reading in the evenings, taking walks by herself. She loved it all, and through her new routine, she'd learned to love the ranch again.

But not enough to stay.

She lay back again, listening to the voices grow fainter and fainter until she couldn't hear them anymore. Her thoughts circled to the letter she'd received from a college in Houston a week ago. Her application had been accepted. All she had to do was enroll anytime before August twenty-fifth. She'd been accepted by an Oklahoma college, too.

Decisions, decisions, decisions, she chanted to herself, then scoffed. What decision? She knew she wanted to go to Houston, but she didn't know if it would be the right move for her.

She should have written Yuri, but she hadn't been able to compose a letter that didn't sound stupid and sentimental or cold and unnatural. Yuri had written her twice and had called once. His letters had been short and a little impersonal, asking her to visit him when she had the time. Maybe he had trouble composing the right letter, finding the right words. Maybe he didn't mean to come off so removed from the man she'd loved and who had loved her until the sun had painted the sky, lifting the dark from the room so that they could make love again in the light of day.

When he'd phoned three weeks ago he'd sounded stilted, as if he were talking to a distant cousin he hadn't seen in ten years. They'd exchanged small talk, spending a half hour on the phone without saying anything important.

She closed her eyes and could see his face just before he'd boarded the van that took him to the Tulsa airport, where a plane waited to take him even farther away from her. She'd lifted a hand in farewell, but he had shaken his head in slow denial.

"No farewells," he'd said, sternly.

He'd looked sad, mournful, heartachingly somber as he'd climbed aboard, sat near the window and stared out at her until the van had pulled away, taking her heart with it.

Missing him took up a good part of her day, every day. Wondering if she should do something about it took up the rest. In retrospect, she found flaws in their courtship. He'd come here under false pretenses, armed with pretty words he'd read in his father's diary. He was a stranger in a strange land who had found comfort in the passion his father had felt for a spirited American woman. Little by little, he had made her accept what had gone before and yearn for it just as he yearned for it.

Maybe it would be best to leave it alone, let it end, she thought. Some things were perfect as they were, and this might be one of them. A perfect union at the perfect time. She'd keep the memory, taking it down from time to time to slowly read.

"Good grief!" She sat up, suddenly in a rage. "I'm not some doddering old woman who has nothing but her memories to keep her warm at night!"

Her love for Yuri crept through her like a cool breeze. It was wonderful to be in love, so why was she fighting it? He was all she'd dreamed of, so why was she pushing him away?

He'd done everything except come back for her and drag her to Houston, and she shouldn't wait for such dramatics. She certainly didn't want to live on the memory of one beautiful night, when he had made a blatant appeal for more.

Yuri had made it clear that night, before his passion had swept aside reasonable words, that he was making love to her, not a dream or a fantasy. Perhaps that was what had brought him to the ranch, but it hadn't brought her into his arms that night. In the darkness that he had professed a fear of, he'd loved her thoroughly, lighting her soul and filling her with an afterglow that she could still feel even after weeks of being without him.

But the glow was fading, and that meant that it was probably fading for him, too. In time, he would forget her if she didn't refresh his memory soon.

She scrambled down from the tree house and whistled shrilly for Honey. Where had she wandered off to? Banner wondered, cupping her hands to her mouth and calling the horse.

Honey came galloping over a rise, hooves flying as she raced toward Banner.

"Where have you been?" Banner asked when the horse broke its speed and stopped a few feet from her. "Down by the pond for a drink, or did you find a berry bush somewhere?" Banner stroked Honey's forehead and saw the telltale blue stains around the horse's velvety lips. "Berries," she said, smiling. "Hope you don't get a tummy ache."

She swung into the saddle and pressed her heels into Honey's side. "Let's go, girl. We've got important business back at the ranch."

Honey flew across the flat land, needing no direction from Banner, since she knew the way back by instinct. When they were within smelling distance of hay and feed, Honey whinnied and her ears pricked forward.

"How can you be hungry after pigging out on those berries?" Banner asked, then wondered fleetingly if Honey would miss her. More importantly, would Banner miss the ranch and the way of life that had been all she'd ever known? Was it fear that had kept her anchored to the ranch even after Yuri had written and called and done everything except get on his knees and beg her to come to him?

Banner swung off the horse, unsaddled Honey and let the palomino into the corral.

"Billy!" she called to one of the stable hands. "Rub her down for me, will you?"

Billy waved, acknowledging the request, and Banner ran into the house as if she hadn't a moment to lose now that her mind was finally made up.

DiDi sat in a rocker near the front door and turned wide eyes on Banner.

"Where's the fire?"

"DiDi, I'm going to Houston. Call the Tulsa airport for me and book me on the next flight."

"All right!" DiDi sprang from the chair, sending it rocking crazily. "Was it his last letter? What did he say?"

"It wasn't his letter. I just realized that I was being stupid. He wants me to visit him and I'm going to, that's all. Besides, I want to enroll in a college in Houston." She smiled slyly. "Convenient, wouldn't you say?"

"Devious is what I'd say." DiDi laughed gaily and went to the switchboard. "Houston, here she comes. Do you want a return ticket?"

"No, let's leave it open-ended." Banner leaned on the counter that surrounded the switchboard. "I'll be back for the wedding, of course."

"Oh, are you planning on staying away *that* long?" DiDi teased.

"DiDi, I don't know what it will be like...seeing him again, I mean. I don't even know if I'll like Houston or that college or anything about it!"

"Don't go making mountains out of molehills," DiDi warned. "Heavens, girl! He's a wonderful man and he loves you. Isn't that enough?" She scowled good-naturedly at Banner's hesitation. "If it isn't, it should be!" She folded her arms on top of the counter and fixed Banner with a stern look. "Let me tell you what my mother said when I told her I was sweet on Pete."

"What?" Banner asked.

"She asked me if he drank to excess, threatened violence or chased women, and I said no. Then she asked me if he had a good job and if all his body parts worked, and I said yes. And then she was quiet a few moments and said, 'Gal, you done good. Marry him.'" DiDi laughed along with Banner, then laid a hand on her arm. "So I'm asking you, does he drink to excess, threaten violence or chase women?"

"No," Banner answered, smiling.

"Okay. Does he have a good job and do all his body parts work?"

"Yes...definitely yes!"

"Okay. Gal, you done good." DiDi turned toward the switchboard, capping the subject. "Marry him."

"He hasn't asked me to marry him," Banner said with a shrug of defeat.

"Hon, that hasn't stopped any red-blooded American woman I know of, so it shouldn't stop you." She glanced at Banner and sighed. "Seriously, Banner, don't make trouble where there isn't any. Smell the roses and avoid the thorns."

The screen door sang out and Pete strode into the lobby.

"Pete, Banner's going to Houston," DiDi said. "I'm getting ready to make her plane reservation."

"Thank heavens!" Pete said, clapping his hands together reverently and looking up at the ceiling.

"What?" Banner huffed, facing him with a belligerent stance. "That's a fine how-do-you-do! You sound as if you can't wait to get rid of me!"

"No, I'm just tired of looking at your moping, hound-dog expression." Pete grinned, holding her by the shoulders and peering at her droll frown. "I know you're scared," he said, lowering his voice to a private pitch and glancing at DiDi, who was busy making the reservation. "But this place will be here if you want to come back to it. I'll keep everything safe for you, sugar."

"Oh, Pete." Banner wrapped her arms around him and hugged him fiercely. "Am I doing the right thing?"

"Yes, ma'am, you sure are. You're following your heart, and that's the best way to travel."

She barely heard him. Her mind had unearthed a snatch of conversation she'd had with Yuri, and his words soothed her more than Pete's could have done.

It's those things we didn't do that we'll regret when our lives are at an end.

Banner closed her eyes, one hand lifting to touch the necklace Yuri had given her. Peacefulness stole through her. Yes, she was doing the right thing.

Ten

Banner sat on a bench across the street from Yuri's condominium, worrying about how he would react to seeing her again. Maybe she should have called first. Maybe she should have sent a cable. Maybe she shouldn't even be here.

Leave a note, a voice urged. Just leave a note telling him which motel you'll be staying in and then let him call you if he wants to see you. If he wants to see you, take it slow and easy. Don't rush him into anything. Men hate to be rushed, especially toward the altar.

She propped her feet on her suitcase and sighed. No, she wouldn't leave a stupid note! If she couldn't write him a letter, then she couldn't write him a note, either!

Checking the fit of her clothes again, she wondered if he'd think she looked sophisticated and urban in her off-white trousers and matching blazer, cream silk blouse and fashionable low heels. She touched the necklace, needing something secure to hold onto, then held onto her breath when she saw a sleek silver Thunderbird glide into Yuri's parking space.

Tears sprang to her eyes—eyes that had yearned for the sight of him—when he unfolded himself from the driver's seat and straightened to his full, glorious height. Oh, he was a sight for sore, heartsick eyes, she thought, rising to her feet and feeling the irresistible pull of him. He was the moon and she was the tide, surging forth in an age-old ritual.

Yuri, Yuri, turn around and look at me, her mind chanted. Turn around and welcome me with your special smile.

Her own smile faded when a woman emerged from the passenger side of the car, a woman of petite build with black hair and smooth skin, a woman wearing a sleek summery dress of pastel pink, and high heels that made her slim legs look all the more attractive.

Banner moaned as her worst nightmare was realized. She'd been replaced.

Her heart wrenched painfully when Yuri placed a hand against the small of the woman's back as they moved up the two shallow steps to his front door. She lived with him! Banner thought with a little sob. So soon. He'd found someone else so soon!

He started to unlock the door, but he dropped his keys and bent over to retrieve them. As he started to rise up again his gaze glanced over Banner, away, then back with the snap of a whip. He straightened slowly as if he couldn't believe his eyes. Tossing up the keys, he caught them in midair with a definitive clasp as his recognition of her solidified and brought a beaming smile to his lips. He started forward, his steps light and bouncy, then he pulled himself up sharply. His smile dimmed like a burned-out bulb, his pace slowed and there was a stiffness in his body as he crossed the street to her.

"Banner," he said impersonally, coldly. "What a surprise." His gaze dipped to her single suitcase, then back up to her face. "Waiting for a bus or did you decide to drop in?"

"I'm dropping in," she confessed, wishing she could find a hole and crawl into it. She looked around, wondering if Houston had caves or grottoes or tree houses. "I should have called first... or written to you that I was coming."

"A letter or a phone call would have been nice," he said, almost snapping at her. "Mannerly, to say the least." He picked up her suitcase and nodded toward his condo. "Come on."

"No, you have company and—"

"Come on!" His hand gripped her elbow painfully and he pulled her forward with him.

She looked up into his face, alarmed by his gruffness, and she saw the dark blaze in his eyes. A slow burn, she thought. He's livid, upset, tense with fury. Obviously, she had intruded on his life instead of being welcomed into it.

The other woman smiled at their approach, tucking her slender purse under one arm.

"Hello," she said in a soft, almost breathless voice.

"H-hello," Banner acknowledged, in a soft, shaky voice.

Yuri unlocked the door and let the two women enter before him. "Banner, this is a friend from work. Diana, this is Banner O'Bryan, the owner of that dude ranch where I spent my vacation."

"Nice to meet you," the woman said, extending one hand.

"Di—" Banner swallowed and tried again, turning wide, unbelieving eyes on Yuri. *"Diana?"* Her voice bristled with accusations. She couldn't believe it! He'd not only found someone else, he'd found another Diana! The man was obsessed! Just as her father had been and as *his* father had been. Diana Dufrayne hadn't been charismatic; she'd been a witch, casting spells on every man in her path and making them love her and only her, wherever they could find her.

Yuri pitched his keys onto a table, then whirled to face Banner, his eyes smoldering with fury. "Yes, Diana!" he said between gritted teeth. "Diana Andrews. You want to make something out of that?" He held up one hand that shook slightly. "Never mind. You already have!"

Diana Andrews cleared her throat, drawing their attention. "Uh...well, Yuri...you were going to get that album for me, remember? If it's too much trouble, I can come back some other time. I can see you two have a lot to—"

"No, it's no trouble." He issued a sharp sigh of impatience and started up the stairs to the second story. "It's in my study. I'll be right back."

Banner stepped down into the sunken living room, conscious only of the other woman—the other Diana. What was this business about an album? Some kind of dodge?

"Look, I don't know what you think is going on here," Diana said behind her, "but nothing's going on here."

Banner turned around slowly and seethed.

Diana held out her hands in a desperate entreaty. "Really. I'm just a friend of his from work. My car conked out this morning and Yuri gave me a lift to and from work. I live down the street." She motioned in the general direction. "I'm a big fan of his father's. I have all of Vladimir Zaarbo's recordings, except one. Yuri offered to loan it to me so that I could tape it. It's all very innocent." She shrugged and looked miserable. "I'm married. Happily, no less!"

"You don't owe me any explanations," Banner said, tossing her purse into a chair and releasing a long, shuddering breath. "And I'm sure Yuri would agree."

"Oh, but I do. I don't want to be the one who spoils this for you or for Yuri." She glanced up the flight of stairs and lowered her voice to a conspiring whisper. "He's been so...so out of sorts since he came back from vacation. He's a nice guy." She smiled warmly. "We all like him at NASA. If you can help him, more power to you."

"Help him?"

"Get his life straightened out," Diana said, as if she hadn't needed to explain. "He's so lost...so lonely." She pressed a finger to her pursed lips when Yuri started down the stairs, then smiled up at him. "Got it? Great. Thanks a million, Yuri. I'll give this back to you Monday."

"Fine. Keep it as long as you like. I've got two others." Yuri handed the album over to her, keeping his gaze deliberately away from Banner. "If you don't get your car back by Monday, just call me and I'll pick you up for work."

"Thanks, but the mechanic promised to have it ready by tomorrow afternoon. Nice to meet you, Banner," Diana said, nodding pleasantly as she moved to the door. "Have a good weekend!"

"Same to you." Yuri opened the door and let her out, then shut it with restrained force. He looked at Banner, leveling her with smoky eyes below straight, lowered brows. "Well, well, well. If it isn't Banner O'Bryan, come to pay a visit and jump to nasty conclusions."

"Yuri, when I heard her name, I naturally thought that—"

"There's nothing natural about your thoughts, *dear*," he said, making the endearment an ugly thing. "She probably thought you had a screw loose when you screeched her name like a warrior's cry at battle."

"I don't care what she thought," Banner said, giving him a dose of her own anger. "You have to admit that I had a right to be alarmed—confused. When I heard her name, I just—"

"Assumed that I was still caught up in some kind of adolescent yearning for a dream woman. I thought I'd convinced you that I wasn't perverted." He stepped down into the living room and across to a portable bar. "Want something to drink?"

"I'll take a soda, if you have one."

"A soda..." He shook his head, momentarily baffled. "A soft drink?"

"Yes. Soda pop. Soft drink. Carbonated drink. Whatever." She threw up her hands and dropped into the nearest chair, sitting on her purse and having to fish it out from under her. "I should have called," she repeated grumpily. "I decided to fly out here and surprise you, but I shouldn't have done that."

"It's been a month." He handed her a glass of soda and his gaze was unrelenting. "A month," he repeated for full effect. "I've written you. I've called you. I've heard not so much as a peep from you. What the hell was I supposed to think?" he bellowed, then spun away from her. "I'll tell you what I thought! I thought that you'd given me the good old red, white and blue brushoff!"

"No, Yuri, I—"

"Let me finish, please!" He glanced sideways at her, his expression downright menacing. "I've been itching to tell you off and I'm damned well going to do it!"

She sat back, folded her arms, and resigned herself to the situation. The dark Russian was in a black mood, and she knew better than to placate him. He tore the pull-tab off a can of beer and drank deeply from it before setting it on the low table in front of the couch and continuing his tirade, pacing before her like a caged beast.

"I don't know which hurts worse: not hearing from you or hearing from you like *that*," he said, flinging a hand toward the door to conjure up the earlier misunderstanding. "I felt like a lovesick fool writing those letters to you and not getting any encouragement from your end. It was as if you fell off the edge of the earth! Houston became Siberia!"

She kicked off her heels and tucked her feet beneath her, setting the glass of soda next to his beer on the table. He scowled at her.

"What are you doing?" he asked.

"Getting comfortable. Looks like this is going to take a while."

He propped his hands at his waist and glowered at her. "Do you think this is funny?"

"No, I think it's silly, but if it makes you feel better, go right ahead and let's get it over with." She extended a courteous hand. "Finish your speech. Tell me off. Vent your spleen." She put up her dukes and squinted her eyes. "Show me whatcha got, champ."

He batted away her fists angrily. "Ha-ha. Very funny. I'm so glad you're amused," he sneered at her, but there was a gleam in his eyes that hadn't been there a moment ago. "Would you mind telling me why you didn't answer my letters?"

"I tried, but I couldn't put what I felt into words. Everything looked like inky blotches of silly sentimentality, and I tore up one letter after another. I started to phone you countless times, but I didn't know what to say until yesterday."

"What happened yesterday?"

"I realized that I was miserable and that the only thing holding me in place was my own fear. Remember," she cautioned, "this is the woman who's scared silly of changes." She sighed and looked around the condo, taking in the decor for the first time since she'd entered. Earth tones, rock fireplace, cathedral ceiling—a house, not yet a home. "We're talking big changes here, Yuri. Monumental, shake-'em-up changes." She smiled, remembering her morning activities. "I enrolled in a college here today. Classes begin in September."

His expression softened noticeably and his smile was brief, but warm. "Good for you. Congratulations."

"I could have enrolled in one of the Oklahoma colleges, closer to home, but I didn't."

He picked up the beer and drank more, then set it back on the table. "Banner, I don't know what I have to do to convince you of my sincerity and clarity of mind. You're the woman I want and I'll accept no substitutes, real or imagined." He shook his head when she started to speak. "I'm a lot like my father. I'll do whatever's necessary to keep you in my life." He stuck his hands in his trouser pockets and wandered aimlessly to the bay windows in the front of the condo. "You're right in a sense. I was infatuated with your mother as she was described by my father. But if I love Diana Dufrayne it's only because she gave birth to the woman who has come to mean life itself to me."

She choked back a sob and sprang forward, stumbling across the room to him. She gathered him close and pressed her cheek against his back.

"Yuri, I love you. I'm sorry for my snap judgments, my hesitation, my inability to tell you how much you mean to me. It seems that I've had to battle ghosts to get here. Vladimir, Diana, my father; but they're not standing in my way anymore. I swear it." Her hands moved up to his chest, splaying across his shirt as she hugged him mightily. "Forgive me?"

He turned around and looped his arms around her neck. His smile wasn't as warm as she'd hoped it would be.

"Forgive you?" He laughed under his breath. "You came here to ask forgiveness? This is a tie at my throat, not a priest's collar." He held her hands and stepped back to look at her. "My, my! No more boots and prairie skirts."

"Do you like my new look?" she asked, unsure of his current mood.

"Yes, but I'll miss the old one." He stepped around her, pulling her with him. "Let me show you my house. This is the living room, and the kitchen is through—"

"Yuri," she said, tugging at his hand and making him stop. "I don't want a tour of your house right now. I want you."

He gave her a measured stare that set her nerves on end. "Ah, yes. But for how long this time? A week? A month? Until school starts?"

"Yuri, we don't have to talk about that now. I'm here and—"

"And I can't stand by and watch you leave, Banner!" His voice cut like a knife. "I'm not going to live as I have the past month. I won't go through that again!" He placed a hand against his chest, against his heart. "I have feelings, too. *I* have fears. *I* have needs. *I* have a heart that breaks and mends and breaks again. You can't treat me like a summer cottage, using me for a few weeks now and then for a change of scenery."

"I'm not!" she argued, alarmed by the depth of emotion he was exhibiting. Is this what he'd been thinking since they'd been separated? That he was disposable to her?

"You're not?" he asked, not hiding his skepticism.

"No."

His hand slipped down his chest, and her gaze followed it then sprang back up to his impassive expression.

"How long are you staying, Banner?" He glanced toward her suitcase. "How long before you return to your ranch...your precious land?"

She rounded her shoulders, feeling the trap closing around her. "I don't know yet. I thought I'd come here and see how things go first. I—I mean, you might not want me to stay. We might not be compatible. One never knows about such things and—" She chopped off the rest when he turned his back on her. He picked up her suitcase and started up the stairs. "Where are you going?"

"I'm putting your suitcase in the guest bedroom."

"The guest..." She ran after him, taking the stairs two at a time. "Yuri, don't be this way! Be reasonable." She gasped when he opened a door and flung her suitcase inside. "Yuri!"

"I'm not playing this game, Banner," he said, his voice low and threatening. "I'm too old to play house. If you share my bed, you share it from now on. If not, you're my guest."

"But I thought you'd want to give this a trial run and—"

"I'm not a used car to be taken out for a trial run and see if I perform well enough to suit you," he snapped at her. "I'm a man, damn it!"

"What do you want from me?" Banner moaned.

"I want you to marry me!" he shouted, jabbing a finger in the air at her. "I want you to take my name and take it proudly. I want you to live here, not visit!"

"And never go home again?"

He laughed scornfully. "What is this? Your tribute to Thomas Wolfe?" He pointed a finger at her feet. "This would be your home and that—" he pointed toward the front door to indicate the ranch "—that would be your summer cottage. Not this place. Not *me*. You'd leave this home and go to the *ranch* for a change of scenery." He sighed and glanced at his watch. "Speaking of leaving, I've got to." He brushed past her and jogged down the stairs.

"Where are you going?"

He paused at the front door and looked up to the landing at her. "I didn't know you were coming and I promised to attend a library board meeting. I'll be back by ten. Make yourself at ho—comfortable."

"But, Yuri, I—" She gritted her teeth when the door slammed behind him. "I think we should talk," she finished lamely. "I didn't expect a proposal, a commitment. I thought I'd have to fight for you, capture you, make *you* see how nice I would be to come home to." She sat on the top step and stared gloomily down the stairs at the front door. "So much for my clever plans."

"Banner?"

Yuri's voice floated up the stairs to her, but Banner snuggled comfortably under the top sheet of his big bed and waited.

"Banner O'Bryan!" he called again, singsong this time.

Banner smiled and tucked the sheet under her arms, wiggled her toes and kept silent.

"Banner?" Worried. "Oh, Ban-ner?" Fretful.

She heard his keys clink onto the table then his jarring tread as he loped up the stairs. As she'd expected, he went to the guest room. She heard him open the door, his softly voiced "Well, damn it." Then his approach to the master bedroom where she lay in wait.

The door swung open, spilling a column of light over her. Yuri stared at her, and she couldn't tell if he was surprised or miffed. He held out his hands and shrugged.

"What does this mean?" he asked, his voice carefully modulated.

"It means you have a naked woman in your bed, and if I have to tell you what to do about it, then you're worse off than I thought."

Her jesting didn't even bring a hint of a smile to his stern lips. He went silently over to the bureau and yanked off his tie, pushing it into his shirt pocket, then he removed his cuff links and dropped them in a brass bowl. He tugged his shirt from his waistband and unbuttoned it, keeping his back to her, making her wonder and worry.

"The last thing you said before you left was for me to make myself comfortable," she reminded him. "So I did."

She watched fretfully as he moved toward the bathroom, stripping off his shirt as he went, then unfastening his belt and trousers. He kicked off his shoes before moving out of her view. The shower came on, filling the silent void. She looked down at the protective sheet, then lifted it to examine her slim form beneath. Not exactly goddess material, but nothing to turn up his nose at!

Letting the sheet float back over her, she closed her eyes and listened to him shower, letting her mind paint an attractive picture of him with water streaming down his chest, stomach, thighs. She twitched restlessly as flames of desire burned between her legs.

When he turned off the shower, Banner was instantly alert, gratefully surrendering the fantasy for the reality of him. Yuri came into view again, wearing a blue toweling robe. He came directly to the side of the bed and looked at her, his gaze moving from her face down the length of the sheet and back up again.

She sighed with exasperation. He'd lost his sense of humor again. She'd only been away from him a month and he'd lost the fine art of laughing at the little ironies that life threw at his feet and in his face.

"Well?" she asked, folding her arms on top of the sheet. "Are you going to throw me out or make love to me?"

"Are you here to stay or just passing through?" he countered, sounding like a broken record to her.

"Yuri, I brought one suitcase because I was afraid you might head for the hills if I moved in lock, stock and barrel!" She glared at his taciturn expression and wanted to slap it from his face. "I wasn't arguing with you earlier; I was trying to set things straight! I left the ranch in Pete's hands and I told him not to expect me back until his and DiDi's wedding. That's in July, remember? This is June. If you want me to marry you and move in here, fine."

"Fine?" he repeated. "Marrying me is...fine?"

"Yes." She shrugged. "I was hoping you'd ask me, but I thought I'd have to get you in the mood." She grinned cunningly. "You know, set the trap. I never believed for a moment that you'd propose—no, *demand* that I marry you the minute I hit your doorstep!"

"Marrying me is fine," he said, doing his broken record imitation again, much to her annoyance. He nodded, turning aside and moving to the foot of the bed, around it, to the other side. "Fine, like a mediocre film or an enjoyable book. That's a strange way to put it, Banner."

"Oh, for heaven's sake!" She wiggled up to her knees, keeping the sheet tucked under her arms. "Let's not argue semantics here! I'm telling you that I love you. I don't want to live at the ranch anymore. I want to live here with you. I want to be a Zaarbo." She gasped, one hand lifting to her mouth. "I never thought I'd say that, but there it is. Zaarbo. I want to be Banner Zaarbo." She giggled, then laughed when he finally smiled. "Has a nice ring to it, doesn't it? Oh, Yuri, don't just stand there. Do something!"

He untied the belt at his waist and let the bathrobe pool at his feet, then reached out one hand and snatched the sheet away from her body.

"How's that?" he asked, his gaze roaming over her ivory skin, rosy-peaked breasts and the dark triangle of her femininity.

"You're doing fine—make that great. Great, like a blockbuster film or a best-selling book."

He laughed and pushed her back on the bed, then slid his body on top of hers, snuggling closer and pressing her deeper into the mattress.

"You're staying," he said, but there was a questionable tint to his voice.

"I'm staying," Banner assured him, running her fingers through his hair before pulling his lips down to hers.

He made love to her with the desperation of a lover who had gone without for too long. Banner rode the crest with him, suspended for a heart-stopping moment before falling willy-nilly into the fury of a passion she'd never known before. It washed over her, drowning her in the realization that she loved this man—this brooding, moody man who had risked everything to come to this country and find her. She gave herself up to the mindless, heart-filling passion that her mother must have felt years ago in the arms of this man's father, and felt not one ounce of doubt or fear or indecision.

Yuri rolled off her and lay on his back, staring at the ceiling as a silly smile of serendipity claimed his lips.

"What?" Banner asked, folding her arms on top of his chest and staring into his dark, glistening eyes.

"They're smiling down at us, I think," he said, glancing at her before returning to his sentrylike gaze at the ceiling.

Banner turned her head to see the shadows above her. "Do you think they're pleased with the way things have turned out for us?"

"Oh, yes." He hugged her closer and kissed her eager lips. "Through our love we've learned to accept theirs."

"Yes, we have," she said, wonderingly. "I can't blame them anymore for what they did. If she loved him half as much as I love you, she couldn't have gone back to any other man, even a good, sweet man like my father."

"Banner," he whispered. "My Banner Bright. You've made everything worth it."

"Everything worth it?"

"Everything I went through, everything I lost, everything I turned my back on when I left Russia. I thought I'd find peace in my work, but I've found it in you." His lips moved along the necklace she hadn't taken off since the day he'd put it around her neck. "I found all that I'd dreamed of in you."

Banner kissed him tenderly, lovingly, laughing softly when he noticed that she was crying. She shook her head, telling him with her eyes not to worry. She was happy. Deliriously, speechlessly happy.

He seemed to understand, for he kissed her back, then held her fast in the dark, which had become harmless and romantic again now that he'd found the light he'd been missing.

Silhouette Desire
COMING NEXT MONTH

IN EVERY STRANGER'S FACE—Ann Major
Jordan Jacks had made his way into Gini's heart years before, but their different life-styles forced her away from him. Whether she wanted it or not, he was back in her life, and this time their desire couldn't be denied.

STAR LIGHT, STAR BRIGHT—Naomi Horton
The only heavenly bodies astronomer Rowan Claiburn was interested in were of the celestial variety. But Dallas McQuaid made an impressive display, and she found this man who radiated sex appeal impossible to ignore.

DAWN'S GIFT—Robin Elliott
Creed Parker fled from his dangerous, fast-paced world for the country life, but his peace of mind was shattered when he saw beautiful Dawn Gilbert emerging from her morning swim. Could Creed's past allow him to accept Dawn's gift of a future?

MISTY SPLENDOR—Laurie Paige
Neither a broken engagement nor time could quell the passion between Misty and Cam. She had left because they hadn't been ready for marriage—but now as man and woman they were ready for love.

NO PLAN FOR LOVE—Ariel Berk
Brian Hollander's "Casanova" style was cramped when he had to play surrogate daddy to his newborn nephew. Valerie knew even less about babies than Uncle Brian, but her labor of necessity turned into a labor of love.

RAWHIDE AND LACE—Diana Palmer
After Erin left Ty her life fell to pieces; then an automobile accident ruined her career. Now Ty wanted her back, for Erin held the key to his happiness. Could she give her heart again to the man who had once turned her away?

AVAILABLE THIS MONTH:

TREASURE HUNT
Maura Seger

THE MYTH AND THE MAGIC
Christine Flynn

LOVE UNDERCOVER
Sandra Kleinschmit

DESTINY'S DAUGHTER
Elaine Camp

MOMENT OF TRUTH
Suzanne Simms

SERENDIPITY SAMANTHA
Jo Ann Algermissen

If you're ready for a more sensual, more provocative reading experience...

We'll send you
4 Silhouette Desire novels
FREE
and without obligation

Then, we'll send you six more Silhouette Desire® novels to preview every month for 15 days with absolutely no obligation! When you decide to keep them, you pay just $1.95 each ($2.25 each in Canada) *with never any additional charges!*

And that's not all. You get FREE home delivery of all books as soon as they are published and a FREE subscription to the Silhouette Books Newsletter as long as you remain a member. Each issue is filled with news on upcoming titles, interviews with your favorite authors, even their favorite recipes.

Silhouette Desire novels are not for everyone. They are written especially for the woman who wants a more satisfying, more deeply involving reading experience. Silhouette Desire novels take you *beyond* the others.

If you're ready for that kind of experience, fill out and return the coupon today!

Silhouette Desire®

Silhouette Books, 120 Brighton Rd., P.O. Box 5084, Clifton, NJ 07015-5084

**Clip and mail to: Silhouette Books,
120 Brighton Road, P.O. Box 5084, Clifton, NJ 07015-5084** *

YES. Please send me 4 FREE Silhouette Desire novels. Unless you hear from me after I receive them, send me 6 new Silhouette Desire novels to preview each month as soon as they are published. I understand you will bill me just $1.95 each, a total of $11.70 (in Canada, $2.25 each, a total of $13.50)—with no additional shipping, handling, or other charges of any kind. There is no minimum number of books that I must buy, and I can cancel at any time. The first 4 books are mine to keep.   **BD18R6**

Name	(please print)	
Address		Apt. #
City	State/Prov.	Zip/Postal Code

* In Canada, mail to: Silhouette Canadian Book Club, 320 Steelcase Rd., E., Markham, Ontario, L3R 2M1, Canada
Terms and prices subject to change.
SILHOUETTE DESIRE is a service mark and registered trademark.

Silhouette Desire

Available October 1986

California Copper

The second in an exciting new Desire Trilogy by Joan Hohl.

If you fell in love with Thackery—the laconic charmer of *Texas Gold*—you're sure to feel the same about his twin brother, Zackery.

In *California Copper*, Zackery meets the beautiful Aubrey Mason on the windswept Pacific coast. Tormented by memories, Aubrey has only to trust... to embrace Zack's flame... and he can ignite the fire in her heart.

The trilogy continues when you meet Kit Aimsley, the twins' half sister, in *Nevada Silver*. Look for *Nevada Silver*—coming soon from Silhouette Books.

DT-B-1

Silhouette Special Edition

Sophisticated and moving, these expanded romances delight and capture your imagination book after book.
A rich mix of complex plots, realism and adventure.

Where passion and destiny meet...
there is love

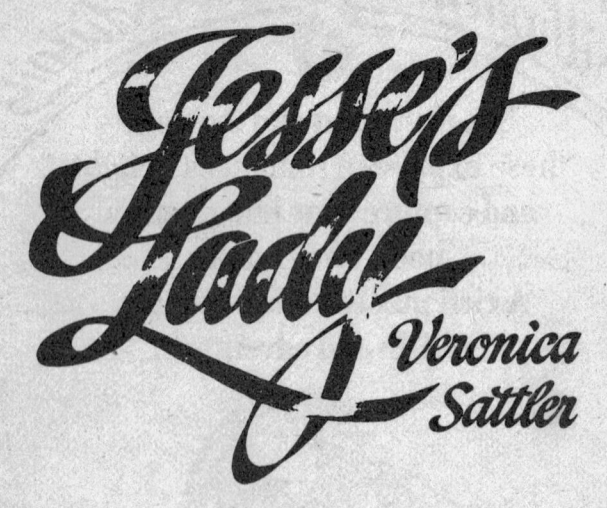

Jesse's Lady
Veronica Sattler

Brianna Deveraux had a feisty spirit matched by that of only one man, Jesse Randall. In North Carolina, 1792, they dared to forge a love as vibrant and alive as life in their bold new land.

Available at your favorite bookstore in SEPTEMBER, or reserve your copy for August shipping. Send your name, address, zip or postal code with a check or money order for $5.25 (includes 75¢ for postage and handling) payable to Worldwide Library Reader Service to:

In the U.S.	In Canada
Worldwide Library	Worldwide Library
901 Fuhrmann Blvd.	P.O. Box 2800, 5170 Yonge St.
Box 1325	Postal Station A
Buffalo, New York	Willowdale, Ontario
14269-1325	M2N 6J3

PLEASE SPECIFY BOOK TITLE WITH YOUR ORDER.